CHEESE

CHEESE

A COMBO OF *OGGIE COODER* AND *OGGIE COODER, PARTY ANIMAL*

Sarah Weeks

Illustrations by Doug Holgate

SCHOLASTIC INC.

All rights reserved. Published by Scholastic Inc., *Publishers since 1920.*
SCHOLASTIC and associated logos are trademarks and/or registered trademarks of Scholastic Inc.

ISBN 978-0-545-93957-7

10 9 8 7 6 5 4 3 2   16 17 18 19 20

Printed in the U.S.A.   40
First printing 2016

Book design by Elizabeth B. Parisi

Oggie Cooder

for my friend, colleague,
and editor, David levithan

1

Oggie Cooder lay on the deserted sandy white beach sunbathing in a green and purple polka-dotted bathing suit he'd never seen before in his life. In his hand, he held a giant coconut filled with the most delicious drink he'd ever tasted, and all around him graceful palm trees swayed to and fro, dancing a hula to the sound of a distant ukulele. A fiery sun hung like a spitty yellow tennis ball overhead. Feeling the need to cool off, Oggie rose in his unfamiliar polka-dotted bathing suit, ran down to the water's edge, and waded in. As he paddled out into the crystal blue sea, the warm salty waves lapped against his cheek and the air was filled with the sweet tropical aroma of dog breath.

Wait a second, thought Oggie, *DOG BREATH?*

He opened his eyes. His dog, Turk, was standing next to him, licking his face. The whole thing had been a *dream*. Oggie wiped the dog slobber off his cheek and looked over at the clock. 7:45 on the dot.

"Good dog," he said, reaching over to give Turk a pat on the head. "You're a regular alarm clock. Except that you're furry. And you have fleas. And really bad breath."

Turk, whose real name was Turkey-On-Rye because that was the name of Oggie's favorite sandwich, barked and raced out of the room, only to return a minute later with a soggy yellow tennis ball in his mouth. He whined and wagged his giant tail, nearly knocking a lamp off the bedside table.

"Okay, okay, I get the message," said Oggie, sitting up and rubbing the sleep from his eyes. "Go get your leash and I'll walk you around the block before school."

And that was how Oggie Cooder, future famous cheese charving champion of the world, started his day.

By the time Oggie got back from walking Turk that morning, his parents had already left for work. They'd gone in early to meet with a plumber about fixing a leaky pipe that had been giving them some trouble at their store. Oggie poured himself a quick bowl of cereal and picked up the mail, which was sitting in a pile on the kitchen table.

"Bills, bills, junk, bills . . ." he said as he sorted through the letters. "Hold on. Is this what I think it is? *Yes!*" He held the long pale blue envelope aloft.

"*Prrrrr-ip! Prrrrr-ip!*" Oggie fluttered his tongue against the roof of his mouth. He always made that sound when he was excited about something. At the moment, the something he was excited about was a letter from the Bakestuff Company about the name-the-new-bagel contest he had entered several weeks earlier. Oggie loved contests, and had been waiting eagerly to hear whether he had won the grand prize — a trip to Hawaii. He'd been dreaming about sandy beaches and palm trees practically every night. Although he had never won anything in his life, he was hopeful that he might actually have a shot at winning the Bakestuff contest. Oggie was very proud of the name he had come up with for a cinnamon-raisin bagel. He had gotten the idea from something he'd overheard his mother say on the phone one day when she was talking to his Aunt Hettie.

"You better warn the neighbors ahead of time, Het, 'cause we're definitely going to be raisin' the roof," she'd said.

"What's the matter with Aunt Hettie's roof?" Oggie had asked his mother after she'd hung up.

Mrs. Cooder laughed.

"That's just an expression, Ogg," she explained. "'Raisin' the roof' means 'having a good time.' Your Aunt Hettie and I were talking about the family reunion we're going to have this summer."

"Is Uncle Vern coming?" Oggie asked hopefully.

Uncle Vern was Oggie's favorite relative. He drove a pickup truck with a jacked-up rear end, and he could make his belly button talk without using his hands.

"Yes, Uncle Vern will be there," Oggie's mother replied. "Which is probably something else I'd better remind Aunt Hettie to warn the neighbors about."

Uncle Vern and his talking belly button were far from Oggie's thoughts now as he ripped open the letter from the Bakestuff Company. "Raisin' the Roof is a perfect name for a cinnamon-raisin bagel, don't you think, Turk?" Oggie asked.

Turk wasn't paying attention. He was too busy sniffing around under the table looking for something to eat.

Oggie unfolded the letter and began to read.

> *Dear Mr. Cooder:*
> *We thank you for your entry. However, we regret to inform you . . .*

"Frappuccino!" cried Oggie in disappointment.

There was no cussing allowed in Oggie's house. Mrs. Cooder kept a big jar on the kitchen counter, and anyone who slipped up had to put a quarter in

it. Oggie didn't see the point of wasting his allowance on expensive cuss words when there were plenty of perfectly good free words you could use instead.

"Frappuccino. Frappuccino. Frappuccino . . ." Oggie grumbled as he read the rest of the letter.

Not only had the people at Bakestuff been unimpressed with the name he'd come up with for their new bagel, Oggie couldn't believe what they'd chosen instead.

"*Sunshine?* What kind of a name is that for a bagel?" he asked Turk. "It doesn't even have the word 'raisin' in it!"

Oggie crumpled the letter into a ball and threw it across the room, missing the wastebasket he'd been aiming for by a good foot and a half. Turk, who was always hungry, trotted over and wolfed down the balled-up letter in a couple of quick bites.

"I guess the only way I'm ever going to get to Hawaii is in my dreams," said Oggie sadly. He shoved his homework and his lunch into his backpack. Then, as he was about to walk out the door, he suddenly remembered something. He went to the fridge, got out two slices of processed American cheese, and slipped them into his back pocket.

That cheese would change Oggie Cooder's life forever. Because while sometimes the road to fame and fortune is paved in gold, there are other times when it's made of cheese. Processed American cheese, to be exact.

2

irectly across the street from the Cooders' house, Donnica Perfecto was sitting at the breakfast table doing what she did best — whining.

"You don't really expect me to eat this toast, do you?" she asked her mother. "It's *burnt*."

"I'm sorry, Cupcake," said Mrs. Perfecto. "I'm not used to that new toaster yet."

"It's top of the line, Miriam, nothing wrong with that toaster," Mr. Perfecto piped up from behind his newspaper. "They really turned up the dial with this one. Took toasty and made it toastier. Most people would kill to have that kind of firepower on the counter."

"Yes, dear. It's just that with the old one, the toast popped up when it was done," said Mrs. Perfecto.

"Popping up is old-fashioned, Miriam," Mr. Perfecto insisted.

Mrs. Perfecto sighed. "If you say so, dear."

"Daddy?" said Donnica, poking absentmindedly at her toast with a pink-glitter-polished fingertip. "This year for my birthday, can we buy a house in Hollywood and move there?"

"*Hollywood?*" cried Mr. and Mrs. Perfecto at the same time.

From the moment she could talk, if you asked Donnica Perfecto what she wanted to be when she grew up, she would say the same thing — "Famous!" Her parents had shelled out a considerable amount of money over the years for music, dance, and acting lessons, but it had become painfully clear that Donnica had absolutely no talent in any of those arenas. Even so, she was sure she was going to become a star.

"Why would we want to move to Hollywood?" asked Mr. Perfecto.

"Well, you don't really expect me to live *here* forever, do you?" whined Donnica.

14

"What's wrong with Wawatosa?" Mrs. Perfecto wondered.

"It's in *Wisconsin*," Donnica said disgustedly, flicking her burnt toast with a finger and scattering a sooty shower of black crumbs across the clean white tablecloth. "How am I supposed to get discovered in a place where the only thing that's famous is *cheese*?"

George Perfecto owned a large discount appliance store out on Stadium Boulevard called Big Dealz. The license plates on the two silver SUVs in the Perfectos' driveway said BIG ONE and BIG TWO. Donnica's room was painted her favorite color, bubble gum pink. She had her own private bathroom and a closet full of expensive clothes, a queen-size canopy bed, and a minifridge stocked with her favorite drink, imported apricot fruit water — which, if you read the label carefully, was actually bottled in Hoboken, New Jersey.

Things were a little different over at the Cooders' house. Mr. and Mrs. Cooder had only one car, an old Volvo station wagon, which had definitely seen better days. They drank their water from the tap, and the whole family shared a single bathroom. With the exception of underwear and socks, which Mrs. Cooder purchased new from Selznick's department store, all of their clothes came from Too Good to Be Threw, the resale shop that the Cooders owned and ran in downtown Wawatosa.

Mrs. Cooder wore exclusively purple clothing, plum being her signature shade, and she was also very fond of unusual hats. Mr. Cooder favored bowling shirts with other people's names embroidered over the pockets. Oggie didn't care about clothes at all. His method of getting dressed in the morning was to yank a pair of pants out of the closet, pull a shirt out of the drawer, put them on whether or not they really went together, and be done with it.

If the pants in the closet and the shirts in the drawers had been ordinary things, like T-shirts and jeans, Oggie might have looked like any other fourth-grade boy who had gotten dressed in a hurry. But since it was Mrs. Cooder who chose the things that went into Oggie's closet and drawers, he sometimes ended up with crazy-looking outfits. On the day Oggie received the disappointing news from the Bakestuff Company, he was wearing blue-and-white-striped seersucker pants and a plaid duck-hunting shirt — complete with a pouch for carrying dead ducks, which, of course, he was *not* planning to do. On his feet, he wore size-11 sneakers, with laces he had crocheted out of colorful yarn.

It was during a visit to Zanesville, Ohio, that Oggie's Aunt Hettie had taught him how to crochet. She hadn't done it out of the goodness of her heart. She'd done it in order to keep him out of her garden. Oggie, who'd been only five years old at the time and bored to tears with listening to grown-up talk, had wandered out into the garden, where he decided to pretend he was on the moon.

He'd imagined that the garden was a big crater, and the birdbath was his rocket ship. Aunt Hettie, spying him out her window, had let it be known in no uncertain terms that she did not appreciate

Oggie moonwalking through her zucchini plants, and she did not appreciate him digging for moon rocks in her potato patch. She *especially* did not appreciate Oggie sitting in her birdbath with one of her good mixing bowls on his head shouting *Blast off!* and scaring all the birds away. So Oggie had explained that what *he* didn't appreciate was that the most exciting thing to do at Aunt Hettie's house was to eat a whole bunch of cucumbers for lunch and then sit around waiting for the burping to begin. Aunt Hettie had laughed and pulled a crochet hook out of her apron pocket.

"Come here, Oggie Cooder," she'd said, sitting down on the porch step and patting a spot beside her. So Oggie went and sat down beside his aunt and let her teach him how to crochet shoelaces. He'd been making them ever since. Some of the kids at school, the kind of kids who are always looking for a reason to be mean, made fun of him for doing it.

"Weirdo."

"Dork."

"Doofus."

"Dweeb."

Oggie couldn't help it that he liked to do things a little differently than other people did. He was who he was. And even though there were times when his oddness made life a little bit difficult, if Oggie Cooder had been anybody *other* than who he was, the extraordinary thing that was about to happen to him never would have occurred.

3

Oggie Cooder and Donnica Perfecto were both in Mr. Snolinovsky's class at Truman Elementary School. On the first day of school, Mr. Snolinovsky wrote his name on the board and made everybody practice saying it slowly a few times. SNOW-LINN-OFF-SKEE. Oggie had never had a man teacher before, although he had noticed that several of his previous teachers had very hairy arms.

In kindergarten, Oggie had been in Mrs. Foerster's class. He had liked Mrs. Foerster. She had pretty blue eyes, wore flowery perfume, and because she had been raised somewhere in the South, when she talked, she had a gooey way of stretching out her words that made it sound like she was saying something nice, even when she wasn't.

On his final report card that year, Mrs. Foerster had written: *Oggie is a very unusual child.* One example she gave of Oggie's unusualness was his tendency to grin when he was being scolded. When Oggie's mother asked him why he did that, he explained that it wasn't because he thought getting in trouble was a joke, it was just that when Mrs. Foerster got mad, sometimes she said funny things. For instance, the time she caught Oggie trying to sharpen a carrot — which he insisted he'd stuck into the electric sharpener by accident, thinking it was a No. 2 pencil — she said, "You can put your boots in the oven, Oggie Cooder, but that don't make 'em biscuits."

Some parents might not have been happy about the word *unusual* being used to describe their child, but Mr. and Mrs. Cooder were perfectly fine with it. They made their living collecting unusual things at garage sales and auctions and reselling them at Too Good to Be Threw. As far as they were concerned, the more unusual an object was, the more value it had.

Over the years, Oggie's teachers had found all kinds of interesting ways to describe him — *unique, quirky, one-of-a-kind*. Last year, in third grade, Oggie's teacher, Mrs. Stifler, had said that Oggie *marched to the beat of a different drummer*. Oggie had found that comment surprising, considering the only instrument he knew how to play was the kazoo, and Mrs. Stifler had specifically told him never to bring it to school again because it was a) incredibly annoying and b) extremely spitty. (Later, Oggie's father had explained to him that saying someone marches to the beat of a different drummer is just another way of saying that a person is unusual, unique, quirky, and one-of-a-kind. Then his mother had taken out the rubber cement and had carefully glued the report card into the family scrapbook alongside all the others.)

Oggie sometimes wondered what Mr. Snolinovsky was going to write about him on his fourth-grade report card. But this particular morning, he was too busy thinking about having lost the name-the-bagel contest to think about much else. As he made his way to school in his seersucker pants and duck-hunting shirt, he noticed Donnica Perfecto up ahead, her bubble-gum-pink backpack slung over one shoulder. She was walking with Hannah Hummerman and Dawn Perchy, two other girls from Oggie's class. Oggie had an idea.

"Hey, you guys!" he called out to them. "Wait up a sec!"

Donnica glanced over her shoulder at Oggie, then whispered something to the other girls. They all began to walk faster.

Oggie started running and finally caught up with them at the corner, where they'd gotten hung up waiting for the light to change.

"I guess you didn't hear me calling," Oggie panted. He was a little sweaty from his run, so he wiped his forehead with his sleeve.

"Ewww," said Donnica. "Guh —"

"— ross!" Hannah and Dawn said in unison, providing the ending of the word.

"What do you want, anyway?" Donnica asked.

"I was thinking, since it's Thursday, which means we've got a spelling test today, maybe we could all walk together and quiz each other on the words on the way."

"Puh —" said Hannah.

"Watch it," Donnica snapped. "*I* do the first syllables."

"Sorry," said Hannah, hanging her head.

"Puh —" said Donnica.

"— leeze!" added Hannah and Dawn together.

Satisfied, Donnica nodded and pulled a tube of cherry-flavored lip gloss out of her pocket. Immediately, the other two girls did the same thing, and all three of them got busy rubbing sticky pink goo onto their mouths.

"Nice outfit," said Donnica to Oggie, as she recapped the gloss and slipped it back into her pocket. "Let me guess — is that from your parents' store?"

"Yeppers," said Oggie as he smoothed the front of his shirt with his hand. He didn't notice Hannah poke Dawn in the ribs or how they were both biting their cheeks to keep from laughing. "So do you want to practice the spelling words?" he continued. "I even made some flash cards." He fished around in his duck pouch and pulled out a bunch of beat-up index cards riddled with what appeared to be tooth marks. "Turk tried to eat them, but don't worry, most of the spit should be dry by now."

Donnica sighed loudly and tucked a loose strand of long, honey-gold hair behind her ear.

"I've got two words for you, Oggie Cooder, and they're both *EEEEW*."

When the light changed, Donnica Perfecto and her glossy-lipped posse stepped off the curb. As they flounced away, Donnica called back over her shoulder, "*Love* your shoelaces, Oggie Cooder!"

"Thanks!" said Oggie, completely missing the sarcastic tone in her voice. "I made them myself."

"Loo —" said Donnica under her breath.

"— zer!" added Dawn and Hannah, and the three of them dissolved in a fit of high-pitched giggling.

As Oggie watched them walk away, he sighed and reached for his back pocket — this would be such a perfect time to charve, he thought. But he stopped himself. He really should study his spelling flash cards once more before he got to school.

The charving would have to wait a little longer.

4

Later that morning at school, Oggie was sitting at his desk daydreaming about how great it would have been if he had won the Bakestuff name-the-bagel contest. He pictured himself strolling into the grocery store and running into one of his classmates. David Korben, for instance.

"Hey, Oggie," David would say. "You sure do have a nice tan."

"That's because I just got back from Hawaii," Oggie would tell him.

"Oh, that's right, I heard about how you won that contest."

Then David would pick up a bag of Raisin' the Roof bagels, which just happened to be on display nearby. "Are these the ones you named?" he'd ask.

Oggie would nod and smile modestly.

"That's pretty cool," David would say. "Hey, you don't happen to be free after school today to come over and shoot some hoops with me and the guys, do you?"

Oggie would have loved an invitation to play basketball with the guys, but it was about as likely to happen as Donnica Perfecto inviting him over to one of her pool parties. David Korben and his jock buddies had given Oggie the nickname Duck because in gym class, no matter what kind of ball you threw at him, Oggie always ducked. And as for Donnica's pool, Oggie had never even seen it, though he had heard kids splashing around in it plenty of times during the summer.

Oggie's seat was directly in front of the teacher's desk, so when Mr. Snolinovsky clapped his hands to announce that it was time for the spelling test, Oggie, who was still daydreaming, was so startled he jumped right out of his seat. Unfortunately, he missed it on the way back down and ended up on the floor in a heap. Bethie Hudson, who sat right behind Oggie, rolled her eyes.

"Remember, class," Mr. Snolinovsky said as Oggie picked himself up off the floor and slid back into his seat, "you are to use each spelling word in a sentence and the sentences must make sense."

He gave them ten minutes to complete the test.

The words they had been assigned that week ended in the letters *o-u-s*. Oggie knew how to spell them all, thanks to his handy dandy flash cards. When Mr. Snolinovsky told them it was time to put their pencils down, Oggie felt fairly confident that he'd done well on the test.

"We're going to try something new today," Mr. Snolinovsky announced. "Instead of marking your tests myself, I'm going to ask you to mark one another's work. Please pass your paper up one seat to the person sitting directly in front of you."

Bethie Hudson groaned and rolled her big blue eyes again. Oggie didn't hear her, though, he was too busy worrying about what to do with his paper.

"No offense, Mr. Snolinovsky, but I don't get it," Oggie said. "You told us that we were supposed to pass our papers to the person sitting in front of us, right? But how am I supposed to pass my paper to the person sitting in front of me when there isn't anybody sitting in front of me, except for you, and you're not even sitting there at the moment, you're standing over by the blackboard scratching your head?"

"Could you have possibly found a longer, more complicated way of asking that question, Oggie?" Mr. Snolinovsky laughed.

"I'm not sure," said Oggie, "but I'll give it a try if you want me to."

Mr. Snolinovsky had been kidding, but Oggie didn't get it. He often took things the wrong way. Either that or he was saying something he shouldn't — like the time he asked Mrs. Stifler if the reason her stomach was so big was because she was expecting triplets. Mrs. Stifler hadn't been too happy about that question, since she wasn't even expecting one baby at the time, let alone three.

"If, like Oggie, you happen to be sitting in the front row," Mr. Snolinovsky explained to the class, "I'd like you to get up and quietly take your paper to the person sitting in the last seat in your row."

There was a flurry of activity as people passed their papers. Oggie got up and carried his test back to America Johnson, who was the last person sitting in his row. America had a twin sister, Asia, who was in the other fourth-grade class at Truman. Oggie sometimes wondered whether Mr. and Mrs. Johnson were planning to have any more kids and, if so, whether they'd be naming them after continents, too. He thought Antarctica Johnson had a nice ring to it.

"You get to do mine," Oggie said, handing his paper to America.

"Lucky me," said America flatly.

When he returned to his seat, Bethie's spelling test was sitting on Oggie's desk.

"The first word is *ridiculous*," Mr. Snolinovsky began. He slowly spelled the word for them: "R-i-d-i-c-u-l-o-u-s."

Oggie didn't even have to look at Bethie's paper to know that she had spelled the word right. Bethie Hudson had great big front teeth that reminded Oggie of piano keys, and she was the best speller in the class.

"Please make sure that the word is spelled correctly and that it has been used properly in a sentence," Mr. Snolinovsky said. "If the person whose paper you are marking has successfully accomplished both of those things, you may place a check mark next to the answer."

Bethie had written: *Ridiculous is a ridiculously easy word to spell.*

Oggie put a big check mark next to Bethie's answer.

Mr. Snolinovsky cleared his throat, ready to move on to the next word, when he noticed that America's hand was raised.

"Question?" said Mr. Snolinovsky.

"What do we do if the person spelled the word right, but the sentence doesn't make any sense?" America asked.

Good question, thought Oggie, until it occurred to him that the sentence America was talking about was *his*.

Oggie suddenly felt nervous. He reached for his back pocket, knowing that a little charving would calm him down. The only problem was, Mr.

Snolinovsky had a strict rule against food in the classroom. Oggie took his hand out of his pocket and sighed. It looked like he was going to have to face this difficult moment without any help from his cheese.

5

r. Snolinovsky asked America to read Oggie's sentence out loud.

"It says, 'Someone is a ridiculous man funny bongo,'" said America.

Everybody laughed.

"That's not what is says," said Oggie. "You read it wrong."

"No, I didn't," said America defensively. "That's what you wrote. 'Someone is a ridiculous man funny bongo.'"

More laughter.

"That doesn't even make sense," said Oggie.

"See?" said America. "He agrees it doesn't make sense, and he wrote it!"

The whole class was really enjoying this. David Korben laughed so hard, he actually snorted.

"Calm down, everybody," said Mr. Snolinovsky. "America, please bring me Oggie's paper."

America, holding Oggie's spelling test by the corner, carried it up to Mr. Snolinovsky, who looked at it for a minute, then scratched his head.

"I'm sorry, Oggie," he said, "but I'm having a little difficulty reading your handwriting myself. I'd like to hear what you wrote. Would you mind reading it for us?"

He handed the test paper to Oggie, who smoothed it out on his desk and slowly ran his finger along under the words as he read: "'Sunshine is a ridiculous name for a bagel.'"

"That doesn't make any more sense than the bongo one," snorted Donnica. She pulled out her lip gloss to apply a fresh coat, instantly causing Dawn and Hannah to do the same thing.

"What do you mean?" said Oggie. "It does so make sense."

"You're cuckoo in the coconut, Cooder," said Jackson Polito, crossing his eyes and twirling a finger around next to his ear.

"If he calls his bagel Sunshine, what do you think he calls his hamburger? Sweetheart?" David shouted out.

Some kids were hooting and clapping by now.

"Quiet down, please," said Mr. Snolinovsky. "Let's give Oggie a chance to explain."

Oggie was grateful for the opportunity.

"Sunshine wasn't my idea," he began. "My idea was Raisin' the Roof, because of the raisins."

"Aww, isn't that nice, he's building a little house for his raisins," said Jackson.

"No, I'm not," insisted Oggie. "Raisin' the roof means having fun, and I figured Bakestuff probably wanted people to think eating their bagels would be fun, right?"

"I'm not sure I'm following," said Mr. Snolinovsky, scratching his head again. "Why exactly is the bagel named Sunshine?"

"Beats me," said Oggie, shrugging his shoulders and shaking his head. "If you ask me, Raisin' the Roof is a much better name."

To the amusement of Oggie's classmates, it was soon revealed that the rest of his spelling sentences were also about bagels:

It was a VICIOUS idea to name the bagel Sunshine.

There is nothing DELICIOUS about a bagel named Sunshine.

It would have been more GENEROUS to name the bagel Raisin' the Roof.

It took a while, but Oggie finally managed to explain about the contest he had entered. Mr. Snolinovsky agreed that under the circumstances, Oggie's sentences, though unusual, did in fact make sense. Not all of the kids agreed.

"Weirdo."

"Dork."

"Doofus."

"Dweeb."

Oggie slipped his hand into his back pocket again and touched the cheese. Boy, did he ever feel like charving now. Donnica Perfecto frowned at him and turned up her pointy little nose. Little did she know that it would only be a matter of time before Oggie Cooder would be holding her ticket to Hollywood in the very same hand that was touching that slice of American cheese.

6

At lunch, Oggie sat at his usual table in the corner next to the garbage cans. The only other person sitting there was Amy Schneider. Oggie and Amy sat together every day at lunch, but it wasn't because they were friends. The way it worked at Truman was that every lunch table had a crowd of kids who sat together because of something they had in common. There was the jock table where David Korben and his basketball buddies sat, and there was the table for girls who liked horses where Bethie Hudson and all her horsey little girlfriends sat. Donnica Perfecto had dibs on a choice table by the window, where she and Hannah and Dawn ate lunch together every day.

There were lots of tables in the cafeteria, but not one of them was for people like Oggie who liked to crochet shoelaces and charve cheese. Charving cheese was one of Oggie's favorite hobbies and, in a sense, Amy Schneider had been the one who'd discovered it.

The Schneiders had moved to town right after the school year began, and Amy was placed in Mr. Snolinovsky's class. On her first day at Truman, when nobody made any attempt to be friendly or invite her to sit at their lunch tables, Amy noticed there were empty seats at Oggie's table. She asked him if it would be okay if she sat there, too.

"Sure," said Oggie, who happened to be eating a piece of cheese at the time.

Amy was painfully shy. Plus, she had a mouth full of metal braces, with a complicated crisscrossing of colored rubber bands connecting her top teeth to the bottom ones in a way that made it difficult for her to open her mouth. She took the rubber bands off to eat, but the rest of the time she had to keep them on. Between her shyness and the rubber bands, she hardly ever talked, and when she did, it was usually in a whisper. Oggie tried asking her a couple of questions that first day to be polite, but it was so noisy in the cafeteria he couldn't hear her answers. Finally, he gave up and went back to eating his cheese.

He was sitting there, absentmindedly nibbling away, when suddenly Amy whispered —

"*Florida*."

"What?" Oggie asked, wondering why this strange new girl was talking about Florida all of a sudden.

Amy pointed at the cheese in his hand.

"It's Florida," she said.

Sure enough, without meaning to, somehow Oggie had managed to bite his cheese into the shape of the state of Florida.

When he got home from school that day, he took an economy pack of cheese slices out of the refrigerator, got the big atlas off the shelf, and spent several hours practicing charving the cheese into the shape of all fifty states.

Charving, a word he made up by combining the words *chewing* and *carving*, was something Oggie discovered he not only enjoyed, but also found very relaxing. That's why, after the nerve-racking experience of having to defend his bagel-related spelling sentences in front of the whole class, Oggie felt that a little charving was exactly what he needed. Sitting there in the lunchroom across the table from Amy Schneider, he was relieved to finally be able to pull out one of the slices of cheese he'd been carrying in his back pocket all day and get down to business.

The reason Oggie didn't keep the cheese in his lunch bag or his backpack was that he had discovered his back pocket was the only place that could be depended upon to keep the cheese at exactly the right temperature for charving. If the cheese got too cold, it would crack, and if it was too warm, it became sticky and hard to handle.

Oggie decided to charve Texas. Some states were easier than others. For instance, Kansas, which was basically a square piece of cheese with the upper right-hand corner chewed off, was about as easy as it got. Texas happened to be one of the most challenging. Oggie had just nibbled down the western side of the state and was heading east toward the panhandle when he suddenly burped, causing him to take too large a bite and ruin the whole thing.

"*Frappuccino,*" he said, tossing the mangled cheese down on the table.

Without a word, Amy opened her sandwich and pulled out a limp, mayonnaise-coated piece of white cheese, offering it across the table to Oggie.

"No, thanks," he told her. "Swiss cheese is no good for charving. Too many holes. Don't worry, though, I have an extra piece of good old American right here," he said, patting his back pocket. "I always carry two."

Amy shrugged and stuck the cheese back in her sandwich, while Oggie pulled the straw off the back of his juice box and stabbed it into the fruit punch a little too hard, causing a stream of red liquid to squirt out and hit him in the face. He stuck out his tongue just in time to catch a drop of juice as it slid off his chin.

Amy covered her mouth and giggled, then handed Oggie the napkin out of her lunch box.

Maybe the road to fame and fortune was not the only path that would turn out to be paved with cheese.

7

After lunch, Mr. Snolinovsky's class always did science and math. Then they would finish the day with an hour of creative writing.

Creative writing was Oggie's worst subject. For one thing, his handwriting was horrible — which was one of the reasons America hadn't been able to read his spelling sentence earlier in the day. But the bigger problem was that Oggie could never seem to think of anything he wanted to write about.

"Ideas are like seeds," Mr. Snolinovsky had explained to the class one day. "Plant a seed and you'll grow a story."

Oggie had stayed after school that day to ask Mr. Snolinovsky a question.

"Where do those story seeds you were talking about come from?"

Mr. Snolinovsky tapped the side of his head. "In here," he said. "And here, too." He tapped the left side of his chest, over his heart. "We're all full of seeds, Oggie."

"You mean like all watermelons are full of seeds?" Oggie asked.

Mr. Snolinovsky smiled and said, "Yes. Exactly."

"That's what I was afraid of," sighed Oggie.

"What do you mean?" Mr. Snolinovsky asked.

"My Aunt Hettie has a garden and she grows watermelons that look like regular watermelons from the outside, but when you cut them open they don't have any seeds in them at all."

Mr. Snolinovsky scratched his head.

"I think I know what you're trying to say," he told Oggie, "but believe me when I tell you that you're a very interesting person, Oggie Cooder. And unlike your aunt's watermelons, interesting people always have seeds in them."

Oggie liked that Mr. Snolinovsky had chosen the words "very interesting" to describe him, but he was not convinced that what his teacher had said about the seeds was true. As he sat at his desk listening to the *scritch-scratch* of pencils going on all around him, Oggie's mind was a total blank. Not a seed in sight. Finally, he raised his hand.

"May I go get a drink of water?" he asked.

Mr. Snolinovsky nodded, and Oggie went out into the hall to the drinking fountain. He took several long gulps of cool water, and when he lifted his head to wipe his mouth, he looked down the hall and noticed a very short man standing outside the school office with a cardboard box in his arms. The man was bald and had dark sunglasses pushed up onto his forehead. As Oggie watched, the man placed the box on the floor, opened it up, and took out a piece of bright pink paper. Then, standing on the box in order to help him reach, he tacked the pink paper up on the school bulletin board. The man noticed Oggie watching him.

"Check it out," he called down the hall to Oggie. "You never know, kid. This could be your big break."

Oggie wasn't sure what the man was talking about. But even though he was curious, he was afraid if he took the time to walk down the hall to look at the bulletin board, Mr. Snolinovsky might notice he was taking too long to get his drink. He didn't want to get in trouble.

"Three o'clock tomorrow afternoon at the Bandshell," the man called, then jumped down off the box, picked it up, and left. Oggie went back to his classroom, telling himself to be sure to remember to stop and look at the pink flyer after school to find out what it was all about.

As he opened the door, he ran right smack into Donnica Perfecto, who was on her way out of the classroom with a bathroom pass in her hand.

"Excuse *you*," said Donnica as she pushed past him.

*   *   *

Oggie had hoped that taking a water break might somehow loosen his brain enough to make a story seed fall out of it. But nothing like that seemed to be happening. Mr. Snolinovsky noticed that Oggie was having trouble and came over to talk to him.

"Can I ask you something, Oggie?"

"Sure."

"Do you have any pets?"

"Yeppers. A dog named Turk. He's the best."

"Does he ever do funny things?"

"Sure," said Oggie.

"Like what?" Mr. Snolinovsky asked.

"Like this one time he buried a bone under my mother's pillow and another time he found a bag of black licorice and —"

Mr. Snolinovsky held up his hand to stop Oggie.

"Write it, Oggie," he said.

Oggie was confused. "Write what?" he asked.

"The story about what Turk did with the black licorice," Mr. Snolinovsky told him. "That's a seed."

"It is?" said Oggie, lighting up.

When the final bell rang, Oggie had already used up two pages (front and back) writing his story, and he hadn't even gotten to the part about Turk throwing up yet.

He put his story in his backpack in case he wanted to work on it some more at home. Then he got his jacket out of the closet, waved good-bye to Mr. Snolinovksy, and started down the hall. As he walked past the bulletin board, he suddenly remembered the man he'd seen earlier and stopped to take a look at the pink flyer. Only it wasn't there. Oggie searched the whole board twice, but there wasn't anything even remotely pink and there wasn't anything that mentioned an event taking place at the Bandshell on Friday, either.

"Weird," said Oggie.

"You sure are," someone said right behind him.

Oggie turned around in time to see David Korben disappearing around the corner with a basketball tucked under his arm.

*   *   *

Oggie stopped at the library before heading home that afternoon. Otherwise, he might have run into Donnica Perfecto and her posse as they stood on the corner waiting for the light to change.

"You guys are coming over to my house now, right?" Dawn said.

A sudden gust of wind whipped Donnica's hair across her face. She quickly brushed it away and then put her hand in her pocket. She felt the pink paper flyer there and pushed it down deeper. She didn't want anyone to see it, especially not Dawn or Hannah.

"I can't come over today," Donnica said.

"Why not?" asked Hannah.

"I've got a stomachache." Donnica suddenly grabbed her middle and grimaced as if she were in horrible pain. "Actually, I think my appendix might be exploding."

"Are you okay?" both girls asked, full of concern.

"I'll be fine," Donnica replied. "But I think I better go straight home, just in case I need to go to the hospital, or anything."

"That's strange," said Dawn as Donnica hurried away, still clutching her stomach. "She seemed perfectly fine a minute ago, didn't she?"

As it turned out, Dawn and Hannah were right to be suspicious. Donnica Perfecto was definitely up to something. The question was . . . *what*?

8

When Oggie walked in the door, Turk went crazy as usual, barking and wagging his tail so hard he actually fell over. Oggie got down on his knees and gave Turk's belly a nice scratch, which set the big dog's tail thumping happily against the floor like a tom-tom.

"Did you miss me, Turkey Boy?" he said. "How about we brush you this afternoon? Would you like that?" Turk's tail was wagging so fast now, it looked like it might come right off.

The phone rang. It was Mrs. Cooder calling from the store.

"I need you to come help this afternoon," she told Oggie. "Wouldn't you know we'd spring a leak right in the middle of inventory? The plumbers had to tear down the whole back wall this morning. It's a mess in here."

"I was just about to brush Turk," Oggie told his mother.

"Well, when you're finished, hop on your bike and come down, okay, Ogg? I'll order us a pizza."

"*Prrrrr-ip! Prrrrr-ip!*" said Oggie, whose absolute favorite food was pizza.

"What do you want on it?" asked his mother. "The usual?"

"Yeppers!" Oggie said happily.

Across the street, Donnica flopped down on her bed and took a big bite of one of the vanilla-frosted oatmeal cookies her mother had set out for her after-school snack. She reached over and flipped open the minifridge, pulling a bottle of apricot fruit water off the shelf and unscrewing the plastic cap with her teeth. Then she reached into her pocket and pulled out the pink flyer she'd torn off the school bulletin board when she'd noticed it on her way to the bathroom.

Callin' all kids.

Hidden Talents
is coming to your town!

We're combing the country in search of kids who can do something cool that nobody else can do. Come show our panel of judges what you've got. The quirkier, the better!

Auditions at The Wawatosa Bandshell. Friday, 3:00 pm sharp!

Donnica still couldn't believe it. *Hidden Talents* was one of the most popular shows on TV. She hadn't missed a single episode of the first season, staying glued to the television set until finally a fourteen-year-old boy from Nebraska beat out the competition to win the grand prize by playing "The Star-Spangled Banner" with a wet hand in his armpit. Donnica was certain that if she could land a spot on the show, it would be the big break she'd been waiting for her whole life. There was only one problem.

"MOM!" Donnica called at the top of her lungs.

"I'm downstairs, Cupcake!" her mother called back.

"Obviously!" Donnica yelled. "But I'm upstairs, so come up here. I need to ask you something."

Mrs. Perfecto arrived a minute later, flushed from her climb and carrying the bag of oatmeal cookies.

"What is it, dear? Do you want more cookies?"

"No, I want you to help me figure out what hidden talent I have."

Mrs. Perfecto put her index finger to her chin and thought for a moment.

"Hmmmm," she said. "Hidden talent? Well, you do have a very loud voice. But I wouldn't say you keep that talent *hidden* exactly."

"Having a loud voice isn't a talent, Mother," Donnica said with a pout.

"What about white teeth? Does that count?" asked Mrs. Perfecto. "You have very white teeth. Which reminds me, I need to make an appointment for you to have your regular checkup with Dr. Schelkun."

"Mom," Donnica said impatiently, "can you please stop talking about teeth and help me think of something quirky that I can do that nobody else can?"

Mrs. Perfecto tried her best, but she couldn't think of a thing.

"There must be *something*," Donnica insisted. "Everybody's good at *something*, right?"

"True," said Mrs. Perfecto. "Your friend Hannah is very good at ballet, and when Dawn plays that flute of hers, she sounds good enough to be in a professional orchestra."

Donnica was well aware of Hannah's dancing abilities and Dawn's musical skills. Their talents, not to mention the talents of various other kids she knew at Truman, were the reason she'd ripped the pink flyer down in the first place. Undoubtedly, other flyers had been put up around town, but she figured anything she could do to keep the competition down was worth it.

"We're not talking about Dawn and Hannah right now, Mother," snapped Donnica. "We're talking about *me*."

"Of course we are, Cupcake. And I'm sure you're filled to the brim with talent, too. It's just that in your case it's extremely well hidden, that's all."

After Mrs. Perfecto left, Donnica rolled over and lay on her back on her bubble-gum-pink bedspread, staring up at the ceiling. She had to think of something, *anything* she could do to impress the judges from *Hidden Talents*. She heard a dog barking outside and turned her head toward the window just in time to catch sight of Oggie Cooder sitting on his porch brushing his dog. The air was filled with floating hair balls.

"Ugh," she said, wrinkling her pointy little nose in disgust.

When Oggie finished brushing Turk, he pulled something square and orange out of his pocket. At first Donnica thought it was a wallet, but when he put it in his mouth, she realized it was a piece of cheese.

Why is he eating it that way? wondered Donnica, pushing herself up onto her elbows in order to get a clearer view.

A minute later, Oggie let out a whoop of joy and waved his masterpiece in the air.

"*Prrrrr-ip! Prrrrr-ip!* Check it out, Turk! My best ever!"

Donnica's mouth fell open. Even from across the street she could recognize the shape Oggie had nibbled his cheese into.

"Texas," she said in amazement.

Suddenly, a lightbulb went on over her head. She jumped off the bed and ran to the window. Yanking

it open, she shouted down, "Oggie Cooder, don't you move!" Then she turned and raced out of her room, flying down the stairs, past her surprised mother, out the front door, and across the street to the Cooders' house.

When she would think back on this moment later, Donnica Perfecto would regret two things: one, that she had left the pink flyer lying on her bed, and two, that in her haste, she had neglected to close the window.

9

Oggie was very surprised when Donnica yelled out the window at him, but not as surprised as Turk was. Even though Oggie had tied the end of the leash around the banister, Turk got so excited when he heard Donnica yelling that he pulled it loose. As soon as he realized he was free, Turk took off on a tear.

"Hey!" yelled Oggie. "Come back here!"

By the time Donnica arrived, Turk was already out of sight.

"I need . . . to talk . . . to you . . . about that . . . cheese," she panted.

"I can't talk right now," Oggie told her. "I have to catch my dog."

Turk shot out from between two houses, a

garden hose clamped between his teeth. When the hose reached the limit of its length, it jerked tight with a loud *BOING!*, sending Turk flying backward into a muddy flower bed. Oggie made a dive for his dog, but Turk was too fast for him.

"Turk! Sit!" Oggie shouted.

Turk immediately sat down and began scooching his backside along the sidewalk — something Mrs. Cooder often scolded him for doing on the hall carpet.

"Guh —" said Donnica, momentarily forgetting that nobody was around to supply the ends of her words.

When Turk made a pit stop at a fire hydrant, Oggie made another attempt to snag him. But again Turk was too quick.

"He's headed for your house!" Oggie yelled over his shoulder to Donnica. "Come on!"

Donnica joined in the chase as Turk went careening around the Perfectos' neatly manicured lawn, knocking over several clay flowerpots and then jumping the fence in a very ungraceful manner.

SPLASH!

Oggie stopped running and looked at Donnica.

"Uh-oh," he said.

Oggie had never seen the Perfectos' pool, but he knew it was on the other side of that fence. As Oggie cooled himself off by running through the sprinkler in his front yard on hot summer days, Hannah and Dawn would ride by on their bikes wearing swimsuits and flip-flops. Donnica would open the gate for them and soon their happy shrieks and the smell of hot dogs grilling would waft over the fence, making both Oggie and Turk raise their noses in the air and sniff longingly.

Sure enough, when Donnica pushed open the gate this time, there was Turk, paddling around in the Perfectos' kidney-shaped pool, leaving a trail of grass and mud behind him as he went.

Mrs. Perfecto came running out onto the patio. "What in the world?" she cried. "Who let that disgusting creature in the pool?"

"Sorry, Mrs. Perfecto," said Oggie. "That's my dog, Turk."

"What on earth is he doing in the pool?"

Oggie was about to launch into the whole story, when Donnica jumped in.

"It's not Oggie's fault," she said. "I told him to put his dog in the pool. I wanted to see if he could swim."

Oggie was surprised. Why was Donnica lying to her mother? He was perfectly willing to take the blame for Turk. But before he could say anything, Mrs. Perfecto turned on her heel and started back into the house.

"If it makes you happy, Cupcake, that's all that matters," she called over her shoulder. "There are clean towels in the cabana banana if you need them."

"Cabana banana?" Oggie asked. It sounded even more ridiculous than a bagel named Sunshine.

"She means that thing," Donnica explained, pointing to a long, yellow plastic storage chest sitting next to the pool. "That's where we keep the towels for when we have guests."

"Oh," said Oggie, who, of course, had never been a guest at one of the Perfectos' pool parties.

"You know, Oggie," said Donnica sweetly, "you really should come over and swim in the pool sometime when it gets warmer."

"Yeah?" said Oggie. "*Prrrrr-ip! Prrrrr-ip!* That'd be cool!"

Turk, hearing Oggie's *prrrrr-ip*, let out a happy bark. Then he continued his pursuit of a large pink-

and-white inflatable beach ball that had blown into the pool.

"So anyway, Oggie," Donnica said, twisting a piece of her golden hair around her finger as she spoke, "the reason I wanted to talk to you was because I was wondering if I could ask you a teensy-weensy little favor."

"A favor?" Oggie replied. "Sure."

"It's about that cheese thing you were doing out on your porch."

"Charving, you mean?"

"Whatever you call it, I want to know if you can teach me how to do it."

Oggie was so delighted he had to *prrrrr-ip* again. Turk didn't bark this time. He'd finally managed to catch the beach ball and in the process had popped it, so he had a mouth full of soggy pink-and-white plastic at the moment.

"Maybe when it gets warmer and I come over to swim in your pool I could bring some cheese and my atlas and we could practice together," he said.

"Um, I don't think you understand." Donnica was getting impatient. "I need you to teach me how to do it today. Actually, like, right now."

"Now? Oh, I'm sorry, I can't. I have to help my mom at the store this afternoon."

"But you *have* to, Oggie. *Pleeeeeeease*," whined Donnica. "If you don't teach me right away I won't have enough time to practice before tomorrow afternoon."

"What's happening tomorrow afternoon?"

Donnica realized too late that she had painted herself into a corner. If she told Oggie about the contest he might decide to enter it himself. She certainly couldn't have that. *Think fast*, she told herself.

"Okay. See, I have to do a birthday party for, um, Dawn's little sister," she said. "They were supposed to have a clown, but he canceled at the last minute. So I said I'd do it. And I don't know how to make balloon animals or do magic tricks or anything, so I was thinking . . ."

"You want to *charve* for them?" said Oggie.

"Yeah. Why not? Little kids love cheese, right?"

"I guess," Oggie said.

"So will you teach me?" asked Donnica. "*Now*?"

"I told you already, I can't do it right now. Unless —"

"Unless what?"

"Unless you want to come down to the store with me. You could charve while I sort shoes."

Donnica swallowed hard. "You mean go *inside* your parents' store? With *you*?" she said uneasily.

"Yeah, we've got plenty of cheese in our fridge," said Oggie. "I'll go put Turk inside and grab some slices. Get your bike and I'll meet you back out here in a minute."

Donnica didn't see any way around it. If she wanted to impress the *Hidden Talents* judges, she was going to have to do whatever it took to make it happen. Even if it meant going with Oggie Cooder to his parents' creepy old junk shop to learn how to charve.

A minute later, Donnica was wheeling her bike out of the garage. As she hopped on, a gust of wind blew through the neighborhood, strong enough to make the bike wobble underneath her. Donnica grabbed the handlebars tighter. Oggie was already waiting for her at the bottom of the driveway. He grinned and waved, then he sniffed and wiped his nose with the back of his hand.

"Dis —" she muttered, as she pedaled toward him. This time she finished her own word, "— gusting."

If only Donnica had looked up, she might have noticed the curtains fluttering in the open window as the wind slipped past them into her room and caught the edge of the pink flyer, lifting it up off the bed where she'd left it and carrying it swiftly away.

10

Too Good to Be Threw was about a ten-minute ride away. Every time a car passed, Donnica would duck her head and tuck her chin into her shoulder to make sure that nobody recognized her. When she and Oggie arrived at the store, they rested their bikes next to each other against the wall. Then Oggie pushed open the door, setting a string of brass bells jingling a cheerful welcome overhead.

"Sorry, we're closed for inventory!" Mrs. Cooder called from the back of the store. "And on top of that, we're leaking!"

"It's me, Mom!" Oggie shouted back. "And Donnica!"

"Donnica Perfecto?" said Mrs. Cooder, pushing her way through a rack of old fur coats and emerging with a moth-eaten sleeve caught around her neck like a one-armed bear hug. "This *is* a surprise."

Mrs. Cooder was wearing a long purple dress with white polka dots. Around her waist she had tied a wide lavender-striped necktie. In her hand she held a child-size felt cowboy hat with a faded picture of a freckle-faced boy on the front. The words HOWDY DOODY were stitched under it.

"Donnica asked me to teach her how to charve," Oggie said, holding up the atlas and the package of cheese he'd brought with him.

"Oh, dear. I was counting on you to do the shoes." Mrs. Cooder pointed to a mountain of old footwear sitting in a heap on the floor. "Your dad's off trying to chase down another plumber, and I've got to move all the hats away from that back wall, because of the leak. Poor Howdy here nearly went for a swim." Mrs. Cooder gently brushed off the cowboy hat. "I really need your help, Ogg."

"Don't worry, I can do both, Mom," Oggie promised.

"Great," said Mrs. Cooder, untangling herself from the coat. "You know the drill. Anything without a mate, toss in the throwaway box."

Donnica looked around and wondered why they didn't just toss the whole place in the throwaway box.

Mrs. Cooder left Oggie and Donnica and returned to the task of rescuing her hats.

"You sit here," Oggie said, getting a chair for Donnica and putting it next to the shoe mountain. "I'll get you started, and then I can match shoes while you practice charving."

Oggie spent about ten minutes showing Donnica the basics.

"It's all about taking little bites," he told her. "Start with Kansas. Kansas, Wyoming, and Colorado are the easiest."

Donnica opened the atlas on her lap and peeled the wrapper off a fresh piece of cheese. For the next hour they worked side-by-side, Donnica charving and Oggie digging through the old shoes looking

76

for matches. Every now and then, Donnica would stop and ask Oggie for his opinion.

"How's this?" she'd say, holding up a lopsided, chewed-up piece of cheese.

"Horrible," Oggie would answer honestly. Then he would put down the shoe he was holding and take a fresh piece of cheese out of the package.

"You need to take smaller bites," he'd tell her. Or, "It helps if you tilt your head when you go around the curves. See?" Then he'd quickly nibble the cheese into a perfect Tennessee, or Oregon, or West Virginia.

"How come you're so good at it?" Donnica asked, tossing yet another mangled piece of cheese into the reject pile that was quickly growing at her feet.

"Practice makes perfect," he said. "But if it turns out that even after you practice you still stink at it, maybe you can buy a book of magic tricks and learn one of those instead."

"Why would I want to do that?" Donnica asked, peeling the cellophane wrapper off a fresh piece of cheese.

"For the party," said Oggie.

"Oh, right," Donnica said. "The party."

The bells on the front door jingled.

"Is that you, Dennis?" Mrs. Cooder called, thinking maybe her husband had returned.

"Uh, no," a woman's voice called back. "Sorry to bother you. I was just wondering if you might have any lamps for sale."

"We're closed for inventory right now," Mrs. Cooder answered. "Plus we've sprung a leak, but, well, come on in. I'll show you what we've got."

Mrs. Cooder came to the front of the store and escorted her customer to the furniture section.

"Sorry about the mess," Oggie overheard her saying. "Plumbing problems. Can you believe one measly pipe could cost ten thousand dollars to replace?"

"Ouch," said the woman sympathetically.

"Heaven knows where we're going to find that kind of money. A lamp, you said, right? How about this nice green one, or if you want something unusual, this kitten has a nose that lights up when you plug it in."

"Oh, that one would be perfect for my daughter's room," said the woman.

Oggie was busy pawing through the pile of shoes, looking for the match to a blue one with rhinestones on the straps, when he glanced up and saw Amy Schneider standing there watching him.

"Hi," he said.

Amy gave a little wave.

Donnica, who didn't want anyone to know what she was up to, was unhappy to see Amy. She quickly shoved the piece of cheese she'd been working on into her mouth, then hid the rest of the package behind her back.

"What are you doing here?" Oggie asked Amy.

"My mom's looking for a lamp," Amy answered softly.

"Oh, well, I'm matching shoes for my mom," Oggie told her, "and Donnica is —"

"Matching shoes, too," Donnica interrupted, quickly swallowing the lump of cheese in her mouth and then jumping off the chair to throw herself into a sudden frenzy of shoe sorting. "We're very busy, Annie."

"You mean Amy," corrected Oggie.

"Whatever," said Donnica. "The point is, we're very busy and there's not much room back here. And besides that, you know what they say about three being a crowd, right?"

Amy got the message loud and clear, but Oggie, as usual, missed the point and didn't understand that Donnica was trying to make Amy feel unwelcome.

"I can scooch over and make more room if you want to help, too," he said. He reached into the pile of shoes and pulled out a red one with a big flower on the toe. "Why don't you see if you can find the other one of these?"

But when he turned around to hand Amy the shoe, she was gone.

"I wonder where she disappeared to," he said.

Donnica shrugged and tried to look innocent.

A few minutes later, the bells jingled over the door as the Schneiders left with their purchase. Donnica immediately threw down the shoe she'd been pretending to find a match for and went to retrieve the package of cheese from its hiding place.

"Can't you lock the door, or something?" she said. "It's very distracting when people just show up uninvited like that. . . ."

In the car on the way home, Amy held the new kitten lamp on her lap.

"Won't that be cute in your room?" asked her mother.

"Uh-huh," said Amy, but her thoughts weren't on the lamp. Instead, she was picturing the sneaky look she'd seen on Donnica Perfecto's face and thinking —

I wonder what she's up to.

11

Later, when Mrs. Cooder came over to check on Oggie's progress with the shoes, Donnica was taking a break from her charving, busy putting nail polish on a pinkie nail, which she'd accidentally chipped on a shoe buckle.

"Dumb, dirty, disgusting old shoe," she muttered under her breath.

"If you're not too busy, Donnica," said Mrs. Cooder pleasantly, "maybe you'd like to give me a hand sorting through some of the dresses on the racks in the back."

"*Me?*" Donnica had no desire to touch clothes that total strangers had already worn.

"We have a lot of cute things. Who knows, you

might even find something you'd like to take home with you."

"You mean *to wear*?" Donnica said, unable to keep from shuddering. "Uh, thanks, Mrs. Cooder, but as soon as my nail dries I really have to get back to practicing. I *have* to learn how to charve today. It's a matter of life and death."

"Life and death?" Mrs. Cooder raised her eyebrows. "That sounds pretty serious."

"Donnica is going to charve at a birthday party tomorrow," Oggie explained.

Donnica couldn't help blushing when she heard her lie repeated.

"Must be a very important birthday party," said Mrs. Cooder, taking note of Donnica's bubble-gum-pink cheeks.

Amy Schneider was not the only one thinking, *I wonder what she's up to.*

The bells over the door jingled again. This time it was the pizza being delivered. "*Prrrrr-ip!*" cried Oggie in happy anticipation.

Donnica wouldn't have minded a slice of pizza herself right then, but when she peered into the cardboard box, she gasped.

"What is that yellow and pink stuff all over it?"

"Pineapple and ham," said Oggie.

"On a *pizza*?"

"Yeppers," Oggie told her. "It's my favorite."

Donnica was about to say something snotty like, "Why am I not surprised that your favorite pizza would be covered with something gross and disgusting that nobody else would want to go near?" But she bit her tongue, reminding herself that she wasn't quite finished with Oggie yet.

"Can you show me again how to make my edges smoother?" she asked as soon as Oggie was done with his pizza. "Mine still look too jaggedy."

At 5:30 Mrs. Cooder turned out the lights and locked up the store.

"Thanks for your help," she said, giving Oggie's shoulder a squeeze. "I'll see you at home. You two ride carefully now, it's starting to get dark."

Oggie and Donnica got their bikes.

"Do you want me to come over later tonight, after I finish my homework?" Oggie asked as they started pedaling along next to each other.

"Why would I want you to do that?" Donnica couldn't imagine actually inviting Oggie to come inside her house.

"So I could help you with your charving," Oggie said. "Your edges are still pretty jaggedy, you know."

"I just need to practice."

"Maybe I could give you some more tips. Like you should tilt your head when you do curves."

Donnica sighed. "You already told me that."

"And you should take small bites."

"You told me that already, too," said Donnica. "Tell the truth — is there anything you haven't taught me yet?"

Oggie had a feeling there was something he had forgotten to tell her, but he couldn't for the life of him think of what it could be.

"I guess maybe I've taught you everything I know," he said.

"That's what I thought," said Donnica, then she stood up and began to pedal harder, quickly pulling ahead of Oggie's bike.

"Hey, wait up," called Oggie. "Where are you going in such a hurry?"

"Hollywood!" Donnica shouted at the top of her lungs, then she rounded the corner and disappeared from sight.

12

The following day, Donnica stayed home from school, pretending to be sick.

Mrs. Perfecto brought her daughter tea and toast in bed.

"Is there anything else I can get you, Cupcake?" Mrs. Perfecto asked.

"Uh-huh." Donnica nodded weakly. "More cheese."

Mrs. Perfecto couldn't believe how much cheese her daughter was eating all of a sudden. What was going on? Had she come down with some kind of strange cheese disease? "You've already had a whole package this morning," she pointed out. "Are you sure you want more?"

"I WANT MORE CHEESE," demanded Donnica.

"Yes, Cupcake, right away," said Mrs. Perfecto, hurrying out of the room.

While Mr. Snolinovsky's fourth-grade class did math and spelling and watched a nature video about the Galápagos Islands, Donnica Perfecto spent the morning hiding under her covers, charving cheese. Once when she was lost in concentration trying to perfect the thumb on the lower peninsula of Michigan, she failed to hear her mother approaching and was nearly caught in the act. Fortunately, at the last second, Donnica heard the doorknob turn and managed to toss the evidence *up* — which is how she discovered that cheese sticks very nicely to a plaster ceiling if you throw it hard enough.

Meanwhile, at Truman Elementary, Donnica's absence did not go unnoticed.

"Maybe she really *was* sick yesterday," Dawn said to Hannah as they sat at lunch together, both feeling at a bit of a loss. They didn't know what to do, with no one there to boss them around or to provide first syllables for them to finish.

Oggie, who was sitting across from Amy, eating a piece of cold pizza left over from the day before, was wondering about Donnica, too.

"She seemed okay when we rode home yesterday from the store," he told Amy, as he picked off a piece of pineapple and popped it in his mouth.

Amy, who hadn't been able to shake the feeling that Donnica was up to something, began pulling off her rubber bands and dropping them one by one onto her napkin.

"Did I tell you that she invited me to come swim in her pool this summer?" Oggie continued.

Amy nodded and, having removed the last of her rubber bands, took an unencumbered bite of her tuna fish sandwich. Oggie had told her about the pool invitation twice since they'd sat down to lunch.

Oggie went on. "They've got this cabana banana thing which is full of towels in case anybody needs one. Isn't that cool?"

Amy nodded. She'd already heard about the cabana banana, too. What she couldn't figure out (and was too shy to ask) was how Donnica and Oggie had suddenly become such good friends. Amy had seen her making fun of Oggie behind his back plenty of times. Why was Donnica hanging out with him now?

"Hey," said Oggie, "I just thought of something. Since Donnica is sick, maybe she'll need somebody to fill in for her at the birthday party this afternoon."

This was the first time Amy had heard anything about a birthday party.

"Whose birthday is it?" she asked.

"Dawn's little sister," Oggie told her. "Donnica's going to charve for the kids, since the clown couldn't come."

"Donnica knows how to *charve*?" Amy asked.

"Yeppers. I taught her how yesterday."

Amy was more convinced than ever that something *extremely* fishy was going on.

*   *   *

That afternoon in class, Mr. Snolinovsky brought out an old record player that had belonged to him when he was a kid. He'd also brought along some special records. There were pictures of cowboys on the covers, some of them with fiddles tucked under their chins, others in bright red snap shirts holding guitars.

"When I was a boy, we used to square-dance at school," he told the class. "Every Friday, at the end of the day, we'd push all the desks to one side of the room, bow to our partners, and allemande left, do-si-do, and promenade until we were red in the face. I loved it so much I thought I might try introducing you to the joys of square dancing, too."

You could have heard a pin drop.

"We gotta dance?" asked David Korben, finally breaking the silence.

"With partners?" whispered Bethie Hudson, her big blues eyes wide in horror.

Oggie was the only one other than Mr. Snolinovsky who thought square dancing sounded like fun. His parents had an antique windup

Victrola in the living room at home, and sometimes they would crank it up and dance. Oggie loved to watch his parents twirl around in each other's arms. His mother had taught him a few steps, but Oggie always seemed to trip over his own feet and end up stepping on her toes.

"Make two lines, one for boys, one for girls, and go from tallest to smallest," Mr. Snolinovsky told the class.

There were twelve girls and eleven boys in the class, but since Donnica was absent, it worked out evenly. Oggie was the next-to-tallest boy in the line, and as it happened, Dawn was the next-to-tallest girl — so they were partners. As Oggie followed Mr. Snolinovsky's directions, taking Dawn by the arm and escorting her to their corner of the square, Dawn shot a look of total despair toward Hannah. Hannah was paired up with Jackson Polito, who she secretly thought was kind of cute, so she wasn't as unhappy about her partner as Dawn was.

Mr. Snolinovsky put on one of the scratchy records, and pretty soon they were square-dancing.

Or at least trying to. Oggie did his best to follow the instructions, hooking elbows with Dawn and skipping around in a circle when the caller told them to "swing your partners!" But it wasn't long before the inevitable happened.

"Ouch!" Dawn cried, suddenly grabbing her foot and hopping around on one leg. "You stepped on me!"

"Oops. Sorry!" said Oggie.

Mr. Snolinovsky told them to sit the next one out so Dawn's foot could have a chance to recover. Oggie sat beside her on the floor while the others continued dancing. There was a lot of complaining going on, but it actually seemed like most of the kids were having fun, even if they didn't want to admit it.

After a while, Oggie leaned toward Dawn and shouted over the music, "You must be excited, huh?"

"About what? Getting stomped on?" Dawn said, scowling as she rubbed her sore foot.

"No," Oggie said. "About the party this afternoon."

"What party?" asked Dawn.

"Your sister's party."

Now Dawn was *really* confused. "I don't have a sister," she said. "I'm an only child."

"That's weird," said Oggie. "Donnica told me she was going to be helping out at your sister's birthday party today. I spent the whole afternoon with her yesterday teaching her everything I know. Or at least I *think* I taught her everything. There might be something I forgot, but I can't remember what it —"

Dawn cut him off.

"Let me get this straight," she said. "You were with Donnica yesterday after school?"

"Yeppers. She came to the store with me."

"*She did?* How did she seem?"

"Fine," said Oggie. "Except her edges were a little jaggedy."

"What about her appendix — was it exploding?"

"I don't think so," said Oggie.

"Hmmmm," said Dawn.

And someone else was added to the growing list of people wondering what in the world Donnica Perfecto was up to.

13

At 2:30 Friday afternoon, as the sweaty square dancers in Mr. Snolinovsky's class pushed their desks back into place and got ready for dismissal, Donnica Perfecto was sneaking out her back door clutching the handle of a minicooler containing several slices of American cheese. She had stuffed pillows under her covers in case her mother came into her room to check on her. Since she was afraid of running into anyone she knew — especially Dawn and Hannah — she'd left herself enough time to ride her bike the back way to the Wawatosa Bandshell.

The weather was beautiful that day, sunny and warm, with none of the gusty winds from the previous day, which had blown the lids off garbage cans and sent all manner of things fluttering and scuttering around the neighborhood.

Hannah and Dawn were standing on the corner, waiting for the light to change, when Oggie Cooder came up behind them. Instead of ignoring him, the way they usually would have, Dawn turned around and faced Oggie.

"Tell Hannah what you told me about Donnica saying she had to go to my little sister's birthday party today."

"That's what she said," Oggie reported. "She told me the clown was sick."

"How weird is that?" said Dawn.

"Very," said Hannah. "She told us yesterday she was going straight home to bed because her appendix was about to explode. But you said her appendix was fine, right, Oggie?"

"Yeppers," nodded Oggie.

"I think maybe it's time for us to go pay her a little visit," Dawn said.

When the three of them reached Tullahoma Street, Hannah and Dawn crossed over to go to the Perfectos' house to confront Donnica, while Oggie continued on home. He knew Turk would be eagerly awaiting his afternoon walk.

A few minutes later, Oggie emerged from the house with Turk on his leash. As usual, Turk had a spitty yellow tennis ball in his mouth and his tail was wagging like a flag. The afternoon walk was his favorite, because often Oggie would take him to the park and throw the ball for him. Oggie glanced across the street, but there was no sign of Hannah or Dawn. He considered going over there himself to tell Donnica that the next time she wanted him to do her a favor, she didn't have to make up some crazy story to get him to do it. He was happy to help her in any way he could — especially now that she'd invited him to come swimming in her pool.

Turk started tugging on his leash so hard that Oggie's shoulder felt like it was about to pop.

"Okay, okay, I get the message," he said. "Here we go."

On the corner, Turk stopped to inspect a large bush popular with the neighborhood dogs. While Turk nosed around in the branches, Oggie turned back to look down the block at the Perfectos' house once more. This time, Hannah and Dawn were standing out on the sidewalk. They waved for him to come over to where they were.

"Donnica's disappeared!" Hannah told him.

"Disappeared?" said Oggie.

"Yeah, her mom is really worried. She said Donnica was acting totally weird today."

"Yeah, like she couldn't stop eating cheese. And now she's missing," said Dawn.

Oggie was about to explain that Donnica might not have actually been *eating* the cheese, she might have been *charving* it — though he was still a little unclear about why she'd want to do that if she wasn't really planning to charve at a birthday party. But any thoughts about Donnica Perfecto and cheese were suddenly lost as Oggie looked down and noticed something that greatly alarmed him. The yellow tennis ball in Turk's mouth had turned a very bright shade of pink. At first he was worried that Turk might have cut his mouth on something, but when he pulled the ball out, he discovered it wasn't a ball at all, but rather a crumpled-up piece of pink paper.

"He must have found it in the bushes," Oggie said, relieved. Then something occurred to him. "You know what?" he said. "This paper looks like the exact same shade of pink as the flyer I saw that guy putting up on the bulletin board at school yesterday."

"What guy?" Dawn asked.

"What flyer?" asked Hannah.

Oggie uncrumpled the soggy paper. It was the very same flyer Donnica had pulled off the bulletin board the day before. The wind had snatched it off her bed and carried it down the street, where it had become snagged in the bush.

"Yeppers! This is it, all right. See? It says: 'three pm at The Wawatosa Bandshell.' That's exactly what he told me."

He held the paper out for the others to see. Dawn and Hannah's mouths fell open.

"*Hidden Talents*!" they exclaimed in unison.

"What's that?" asked Oggie.

"It's only the hottest show on TV right now," Dawn explained.

"Everybody watches it," Hannah added.

Everybody but Oggie. He'd never even heard of *Hidden Talents*, which was not all that surprising considering that the Cooders didn't own a television set. Mr. and Mrs. Cooder firmly believed that microwave ovens, hair spray, diet soda, and television were all very bad for your brain cells, so they didn't allow any of those things in their home.

"Donnica's not missing," said Hannah, looking carefully at the flyer.

"She's not?" asked Dawn.

"No," Hannah said. "And she's not sick, either."

"Then where is she?" asked Oggie.

"She's *auditioning*," said Hannah.

"Why didn't she tell us about the audition?" Dawn sounded hurt.

"Probably because she was afraid we might beat her," said Hannah. "What time is it, anyway?"

Oggie looked at his watch. "Ten after three."

The front door opened and Mrs. Perfecto came rushing out of the house with her car keys in her hand.

"I've got to go look for my Cupcake," she cried.

"We've got a pretty good idea about where she is," Dawn told her.

"You do? Oh, thank goodness!" Mrs. Perfecto put her hand over her heart. She opened the side door of the SUV.

"Jump in. You can help me find her. Oh, I hope she's all right!"

"She may not be once I get my hands on her," muttered Dawn as she and Hannah climbed into the car.

Oggie wasn't sure if he was invited, too, but Turk, who loved nothing better than a ride in the car, bounded into the backseat, dragging Oggie along with him.

Five minutes later, Mrs. Perfecto was turning into the parking lot of the Bandshell.

"Are you sure this is where she is?" she asked.

Oggie looked across the lawn at the small crowd gathered in front of the stage.

"There she is!" he said, pointing at a figure in pink corduroy overalls, standing on the side of the stage pacing nervously.

"Cupcake!" cried Mrs. Perfecto.

"What's she holding?" asked Hannah, squinting at Donnica as she tried to make out what was in her hand.

"Looks like a book," said Dawn. "Or maybe a CD."

But Oggie shook his head. He knew exactly what it was.

"Cheese," he told them all.

14

As the four of them got out of the car and hurried toward the Bandshell, Mrs. Perfecto and the two girls peppered Oggie with enough questions so that by the time they reached the stage they were all aware of what Donnica was planning to do with the piece of cheese in her hand.

"She's stealing your talent, Oggie," someone said softly.

But it wasn't Mrs. Perfecto or Dawn or Hannah who said it. It was Amy Schneider.

"Where did you come from?" Oggie asked, surprised.

"I had a feeling Donnica was up to no good," Amy told him. "So when I saw her ride by my house on her bike a little while ago, I followed her here. I just hope we're not too late."

"Too late for what?" asked Oggie.

"To stop her."

"Next!" cried a small bald man with a large megaphone.

"Hey! That's the flyer guy," said Oggie, pointing to the man.

Donnica walked out onto the stage and stood in front of the judges, who were sitting in a row of metal folding chairs behind a long table.

"State your name and your hidden talent for the judges, please," the man with the megaphone said.

Donnica flashed the judges her biggest, brightest smile.

"My name is Donnica Perfecto and my hidden talent is *charving*."

"Excuse me? Did you say *carving*?" asked one of the judges leaning forward.

"No," said Donnica. "*Charving*. It's a combination of chewing and carving."

"Quirky," said the judge, nodding approvingly.

Donnica flashed another smile.

"Aren't you going to stop her?" asked Amy, giving Oggie a little nudge toward the stage.

"Why would I do that?"

"Because she stole your talent," said Amy.

"No, she didn't," said Oggie. "I taught her how to charve."

"But she tricked you," Hannah chimed in.

"And she lied to us," added Dawn.

"Doesn't she look lovely?" sighed Mrs. Perfecto, who seemed to have completely forgotten that only minutes ago she'd been worried sick about her daughter's whereabouts.

"Quiet, please!" the man shouted at the crowd through his megaphone. Then he turned back to Donnica and said, "You're on, kid."

Donnica flashed that smile again, then she lifted the cheese to her lips dramatically.

"Wisconsin!" she announced. But before she'd even taken a bite, she stopped.

"Something's not right," she said, looking at the cheese. "There's something wrong with this piece. It's *sticky*."

"Too warm," Oggie told Amy. "She shouldn't have held it in her hand for so long before she started."

"Hang on," Donnica told the judges. "I'll get another piece."

She ran over to the side of the stage where she'd stashed her minicooler. Flipping it open, she quickly grabbed a fresh slice of cheese, tore off the cellophane wrapper with her teeth, and hurried back to her spot.

"Wisconsin!" she announced again. But this time when she bit into the cheese, it cracked in half.

"Too cold," said Oggie.

"What's happening?" asked Mrs. Perfecto nervously.

"Justice," whispered Dawn.

"Yeah," agreed Hannah with a satisfied smile.

The man with the megaphone was growing

impatient. "Sorry, kid," he said. "Your time's up. We've got a schedule to keep to here. Who's next?"

Amy was relieved that Donnica wasn't going to get away with her little plan, but when she turned to Oggie to tell him so, she found he wasn't standing next to her anymore. Looking up, she was surprised to see him running out onto the stage.

"Hey, Donnica!" Oggie shouted as he sprinted across the stage, pulling Turk along behind him on his leash. "I finally remembered what I forgot to tell you before. The cheese has to be the right temperature!" He pulled a slice of cheese out of his back pocket and waved it in the air. "Like this one!"

"Gimme that!" screamed Donnica, reaching for the cheese with a desperate look in her eyes.

But as Oggie ran past the judge's table, Turk caught a whiff of the crusts of a roast beef sandwich one of them had left lying on a paper plate after lunch, and he took a sudden unexpected detour. Oggie tripped over the leash and his feet came out from under him, causing him to fall just as he reached Donnica.

"Ooomph!"

"Youch!"

The two collided, bumping heads so hard they both saw stars and landed in a tangle of arms and legs on the stage.

Donnica's processed American ticket to Hollywood flew out of Oggie's hand, sailing high up into the air. It looked like the audition was over, but then to everyone's amazement, Donnica managed to untangle herself in time to leap up and catch the cheese a split second before it hit the floor.

"Wait!" she shouted, rushing back to face the judges.

The man with the megaphone took pity on her. "One last chance, kid."

"With-consin!" said Donnica, holding up the cheese.

Dawn looked at Hannah. "Is it my imagination, or did she just say 'With-consin'?"

15

Thanks to the perfect climate in Oggie's back pocket, the cheese finally cooperated. Donnica felt certain that the judges would be impressed by Wisconsin, and so she had practiced it many times up in her room. Now she closed her eyes to help her concentrate, and carefully began to nibble the cheese, taking tiny bites and tilting her head as she went around the curves, just the way Oggie had taught her.

Oggie stayed right where he was, afraid if he got up and left in the middle of Donnica's performance it might distract the judges or, worse, mess Donnica up. In the excitement, Turk had managed to grab the sandwich crusts and run off with them. To Oggie's relief, he saw that Amy had caught Turk before he'd gotten very far and was holding tight to his leash now.

As he watched Donnica charve, Oggie could tell that she'd been practicing because she was much more confident than she'd been the day before. The judges leaned forward with great interest. They seemed to be enjoying it. Oggie felt proud of his pupil. Then as Donnica turned the cheese in her hands, Oggie caught a glimpse of what looked like a very jaggedy edge and suddenly he felt nervous for her. Without thinking about it, he did what he always did when he felt nervous. He reached into his back pocket, pulled out the remaining slice of cheese, and began to charve to calm his nerves.

Donnica finished, opened her eyes, and held up her cheese triumphantly. Oggie's heart sank when he saw it. Just as he'd suspected, it was jaggedy. Really jaggedy. In fact, it was the worst job of charving he'd ever seen her do. But while he was sitting there feeling sorry for her, the judges suddenly broke into enthusiastic applause.

"First-rate!"

"Dynamite talent!"

"Quirky with a capital *Q*!" one of them exclaimed enthusiastically.

"Fank you," said Donnica, taking a bow.

This time it was Hannah who looked at Dawn. "*Fank* you?"

"No, no, not you, honey," one of the judges said to Donnica. "We're talking about *him*."

Shocked, Donnica whirled around on her heel to see who they were pointing at . . . and there was Oggie Cooder holding a perfectly charved Texas in his hand. Donnica was so angry her face turned a shade of purple Mrs. Cooder would have called *eggplant*.

"Thath not fair!" she wailed. "I wath thuppothed to be the one audithioning."

There was a sudden gasp from the audience as Mrs. Perfecto pointed at Donnica with a shaking finger.

"Your teeth, Cupcake! What's happened to your beautiful teeth?"

Donnica quickly put her fingers up to her mouth.

No wonder the charving had been off! She had chipped both of her front teeth when she and Oggie had bumped heads! Needless to say, she was furious.

"I won't forget thith, Oggie Cooder!" she shouted before she ran off the stage.

Mrs. Perfecto quickly whisked Donnica away in the SUV for an emergency dental appointment with Dr. Schelkun. Oggie felt terrible. He hadn't meant to ruin Donnica's audition. He even tried to persuade the judges to give her another chance.

"Maybe she could come back tomorrow and charve for you after she gets her teeth fixed," he said. "She's usually much better than that, and she's been practicing a lot."

"There's only one slot left for the next show, and we have to fill it today," they told Oggie.

"But —" said Oggie.

"Sorry kid," said the man with the megaphone.

So Oggie, feeling miserable and guilty, slunk off the stage.

"Thanks for watching Turk," he said as Amy handed him back the leash. "I guess I'd better get going."

"You can't leave now," Amy told him.

"Why not?" said Oggie.

"Because you don't know yet whether you won," she answered.

"I never win anything," Oggie said. "And I didn't even mean to audition, I was just charving because I felt nervous for Donnica."

Up on the stage, Mr. Megaphone gestured to a boy with a large, white rabbit under his arm.

"You're next, kid. State your name and your talent for the judges, please."

"My name is Fred McMinnville, and I can make my rabbit faint," the boy told them.

The judges smiled and nodded their approval.

Fred set the rabbit down on the stage, crouched down beside it, and blew in its face. The rabbit instantly fell over in a dead faint.

Turk started barking so excitedly that Oggie had

to shush him. One of the judges asked Fred how he'd done the trick.

"Onion breath," he said, pulling a large red onion out of his pocket and taking a big bite of it. "Works every time."

"That was a pretty neat trick," Oggie said to Amy. "I wonder if it would work on Turk."

Next up was a little redheaded girl with a jar of olives in her hand.

"I can tap dance and eat olives at the same time," she announced proudly.

The judges didn't seem all that impressed, but Turk loved her because she kept dropping the olives, which he would gobble down as they rolled off the edge of the stage. One by one, kids came out and did strange, quirky things. There was a boy who could make his ears disappear by folding them up and tucking them inside his ear holes, and a tall skinny girl who could pop balloons with her shoulder blades. There were a number of kids who did tricks with hula hoops, including one girl who nearly choked herself by putting the hoop around her neck and trying to keep it going while she did an impression of the sound of a toilet flushing. When the last of the auditions were over, the judges bent their heads together and began to whisper. After a while, they called Fred back up and asked whether the fainting rabbit trick really worked every time.

"Well, almost every time," he said. "Sometimes, though, he just sneezes."

"Where's the kid with the cheese?" called the man with the megaphone.

"See? I told you," said Amy excitedly.

Oggie was called up onto the stage and asked whether Texas was the only state he could charve. Oggie didn't want to brag, but of course he told the truth, admitting that he could do all fifty.

"How about instead of one particular state, if we asked you to charve the entire country, do you think you could do that?" said one of the judges.

Oggie thought for a second.

"Well, I've never done it before," he said. "But I'm willing to give it a try. There's one problem though —" Oggie patted his back pocket. "I'm out of cheese."

It was Amy who noticed the minicooler Donnica had left behind. She ran and got a slice of cheese out of it and brought it to Oggie. He made sure to warm it up a little before he began to charve.

A minute later, everyone was very impressed when Oggie held up a perfectly executed U.S. of A.

Again the judges bent their heads together and whispered. This time they came to a decision.

"Pack your cheese, Oggie Cooder. You're going to Hollywood!"

16

What happened after that was all kind of a blur. News traveled fast, and the next morning Oggie's face was on the front page of the Wawatosa newspaper with the headline "LOCAL BOY BECOMES BIG CHEESE!" A television crew was outside on the Cooders' front lawn when Oggie came out to take Turk for his morning walk. Reporters began firing questions at him.

"How old were you when you first started charving?"

"When do you leave for Hollywood?"

"What are you going to do with the money?"

"What money?" asked Oggie.

"Didn't anyone tell you?" said one of the reporters. "Everybody who goes on the show gets ten thousand dollars. And if you win the whole she-bang, well, then we're talking *really* big bucks."

"Ten thousand dollars?" said Oggie. "Are you sure about that?"

"That's right. Ten thou."

"*Prrrrr-ip! Prrrrr-ip!*" cried Oggie happily, because he knew *exactly* what he was going to do with the money.

By noon, Oggie had received calls from a dozen different cheese companies asking if he'd be willing to use their product when he went on the show. Oggie's Aunt Hettie called to congratulate him and to say she'd always known he was destined for greatness. The Cooders were very proud of their son, and Mrs. Cooder carefully glued the newspaper clipping about Oggie into the scrapbook. Oggie had entered more contests than he could count, but this was the first time he had ever won anything. He should have been *prrrrr-ip*ing happily all over the place. But the one problem was — he felt bad about Donnica.

The Cooders had called the Perfectos immediately when they heard about Donnica's teeth,
insisting on paying half of the dental bills. But
Oggie knew that Donnica's chipped teeth were
only part of the reason she was mad at him. She
had wanted to win herself, and even though she had
tricked Oggie into teaching her how to charve, he
still felt guilty that he was the one who was going
to be going to Hollywood. He wished he could
think of something he could do to make it up to
her, but so far the only idea he'd come up with
was to crochet her a pair of shoelaces, which he
planned to do as soon as he could get his hands on
some pink yarn.

Later that day, Oggie was out in the garage
pumping up his bicycle tires, when a shadow fell
across the floor. At first, he thought maybe it was
another reporter coming to ask him more questions, but when he looked up, there was Donnica
Perfecto.

"Oh, hi," said Oggie. "How are your teeth
feeling?"

"I'm not here to talk about my teeth," Donnica told him. There was a gleam in her eye that made Oggie feel uncomfortable.

She wasn't a big girl, but Donnica looked pretty strong. Oggie thought there was a distinct possibility that he was about to get flattened.

"Are you ready, Oggie Cooder?" Donnica asked.

"Not really," Oggie answered truthfully.

"Well, get ready, because when I'm done with you, even your own mother's not going to be able to recognize you."

Donnica Perfecto did not flatten Oggie in his garage that afternoon. What she did do was offer him a deal.

"I'll forgive you for what you did if you let me be your manager."

Truthfully, Oggie had no idea what a manager might do, but he didn't care. As soon as he heard the word "forgive," he was sold on the idea.

"*Prrrrr-ip! Prrrrr-ip!*" he said, relieved to be off the hook.

"I'm going to assume that ridiculous noise you're making means we have a deal," said Donnica.

"Yeppers!" agreed Oggie happily. "And now I don't even have to find pink yarn!"

When Oggie Cooder walked into Mr. Snolinovsky's classroom on Monday morning, everybody was excited to see him. People who didn't normally even say hello came running over to clap him on the back.

"I saw you in the newspaper!"

"Everybody's talking about you!"

"Hey, Oggie," giggled America Johnson, holding out two pieces of paper she had ripped from her notebook. "Can I have your autograph? One for me and one for my sister?"

Donnica jumped in before Oggie could answer.

"No autographs," she commanded. "And no pictures."

"Says who?" asked America.

"Says me," Donnica answered.

"Who made you boss?" David Korben asked.

"*He* did," said Donnica, jerking a thumb in Oggie's direction. "Right, Oggie?"

Oggie shrugged his shoulders and grinned. He couldn't believe how much his life had changed all because of one little piece of cheese.

At lunch, Donnica insisted that Oggie sit with her at the table by the window.

"Hurry up and eat," she said as Oggie unwrapped his sandwich. "We need to practice."

Donnica had taken to carrying a stopwatch with her so she could time Oggie when he practiced his charving.

"I still don't understand why I have to do it fast," Oggie said. "I didn't do it fast at the audition."

"You want to win, don't you?" Donnica told him.

Oggie nodded.

"You know that kid I told you about who won last year?" Donnica continued. "The one who could play 'The Star-Spangled Banner' with his armpit? Well, you wouldn't believe how fast he did it. And the judges *loved* him. And the kid who cracked the walnuts with his toes? He might have won instead if somebody had told him to speed it up a little. Now hurry up and finish your lunch — we've got work to do."

Having no interest any longer in being any-where near Donnica Perfecto, Dawn and Hannah joined Amy at Oggie's old table over by the garbage cans. The three girls watched Donnica fussing over Oggie.

"Can you believe it?" Dawn said. "A few days ago she was calling him a loser, and now she's acting like she owns him or something."

"I can't believe we used to like her," said Hannah. "She's so fake."

"Yeah, like why is she helping Oggie try to win?" Dawn wondered. "We were her best friends and she didn't even tell us about the audition."

Amy didn't say anything. She just looked across the room at Oggie and shook her head. He wasn't the only one having a hard time believing how much that piece of cheese had changed things.

17

"here are your glasses?" Donnica asked Oggie as they walked down the hall to the classroom after lunch.

"In my pocket," Oggie answered.

"Put them on," Donnica said, snapping her fingers at him.

"But they're sunglasses," he pointed out.

"Trust me, people in Hollywood always wear sunglasses, even when they're inside."

"But we're not in Hollywood."

Donnica gave him her *don't cross me* look, something Oggie had been seeing quite a lot of since Donnica had become his manager. In order to avoid a confrontation, he put the sunglasses on.

David and a couple of his jock buddies sidled over to them.

"Hey, Oggie," David said. "How about playing a little B-ball with us after school? Maybe the newspaper will come and take our pictures."

Oggie was thrilled.

"Prrrrr-ip! Prrrrr-ip!"

"STOP *prrrrr-ip*ing!" Donnica demanded, grabbing Oggie's arm. "How many times do I have to tell you, that noise is annoying and weird. Trust me, Hollywood does not like annoying and weird."

"What about it, Oggie? Want to play ball with us?" asked David again. "You don't have to listen to everything old bossy face says."

"Oh, yes, he does!" said Donnica. "And there is absolutely no way he can play basketball this afternoon."

"Why not?" Oggie asked, dismayed.

"A, we have too much work to do. And B, you might do something cloddy, like run into somebody and chip your teeth," Donnica told Oggie pointedly.

So Oggie reluctantly declined an invitation he'd basically been waiting for his whole life.

After school, Donnica insisted that Oggie go with her to Selznick's department store.

"You need some new clothes," she told him.

"What's wrong with the clothes I've already got?" asked Oggie.

"You want to win, don't you?" said Donnica. "Trust me, your clothes are too weird. And one other thing — you know that silly word you always say instead of yes?"

"You mean 'yeppers'?" said Oggie. "What about it?"

"People in Hollywood don't say 'yeppers,' they just say yes. Understood?"

"Yes," said Oggie quietly, and he noticed the first small twinges of an uncomfortable pinching feeling in the pit of his stomach.

Donnica Perfectos' ideas about fashion boiled down to the complete opposite of everything Oggie had ever worn.

She picked out a pair of khaki pants and a navy blue polo shirt for him to try on.

"I like stripes," Oggie told her. "And checks, too."

"No stripes," said Donnica. "And absolutely no checks. Put these on and then we'll go look for shoes. You'll need brown ones to go with your pants."

"I've got some brown yarn," Oggie told Donnica. "Maybe I'll make some laces to go with my new shoes."

"You're not going to wear homemade shoelaces on the show," said Donnica.

"I'm not?" asked Oggie. He couldn't imagine wearing shoes without homemade laces in them.

"No," said Donnica, "because —"

"People in Hollywood don't wear crocheted shoelaces?" guessed Oggie.

"True," Donnica said, "but the main reason is because they look dumb."

Oggie was confused. "The other day you told me you loved them. Remember? You said, 'Love your shoelaces, Oggie Cooder.'"

"I was kidding," said Donnica as they turned the corner and started up Tullahoma Street.

Oggie put his hand on his stomach. That uncomfortable pinching feeling was getting a little bit stronger.

"What's the matter with you?" asked Donnica, noticing Oggie rubbing his stomach.

"I'm not sure," said Oggie. "You don't think my appendix is about to explode, do you?"

Donnica didn't answer. She was looking up the street at Oggie's house.

"Whose car is that in your driveway?" she asked.

Oggie told her he didn't recognize it.

"Well, if it's anybody important, call me," Donnica said. "And remember —"

"I know." Oggie sighed, rubbing his stomach again. "No autographs, no photographs, no basketball, no shoelaces, no nothing."

There were two men sitting in the living room with Mrs. Cooder when Oggie walked in. Turk came charging over to jump up on Oggie and give him a welcome-home face licking.

"So this is the famous Oggie Cooder everyone's been talking about," said the taller of the two men, rising in order to shake Oggie's hand. He had on blue jeans and a white shirt with the sleeves rolled up. On his feet he wore expensive-looking leather loafers and no socks. "I'm Bradley Mathis from *HT*."

"What's *HT*?" asked Oggie.

The man chuckled. "*Hidden Talents*. You have heard of the show, haven't you?"

"Actually none of us were familiar with your show until Oggie got chosen to be on it," said Mrs. Cooder, smoothing the front of her purple skirt with her hand. "You see, we don't own a television, Mr. Mathis."

Mr. Mathis looked stunned.

"Do you mean to say, you've never seen the show?" he asked Oggie.

"No, I haven't," said Oggie. "Does that mean I can't be on it?"

"Are you kidding?" exclaimed Mr. Mathis. "Our publicity people are going to *love* this!" He pulled a pen out of his pocket. "I've brought some contracts for you and your parents to sign, and Jimmy here is going to snap a few photos."

The other man unsnapped the black bag hanging from his shoulder and pulled out a camera.

"I'm not supposed to sign anything or have my picture taken without my manager here," said Oggie, remembering Donnica's rules. "And I can't play basketball with you, either."

"You have a manager?" Mr. Mathis seemed surprised. "That was fast. What agency?"

"It's just the neighbor girl," Mrs. Cooder explained. "She's taken a sudden and rather surprising interest in Oggie since you people came to town."

"Yeah," Oggie said, "she's the one who bought me these new clothes."

"I was wondering where those came from," said Mrs. Cooder, eyeing Oggie's crisp new khaki pants.

"Actually," said Mr. Mathis, "I was wondering about those clothes myself. Do you think I could talk to that manager of yours, Oggie?"

"Hang on," said Oggie. "I know how to get her over here fast."

He walked over to the window, pulled it open, and leaned out.

"DONNICA!" he shouted. "Somebody's trying to take my picture!"

Two seconds later, she was there.

18

Apparently, Donnica knew a lot less about Hollywood than she thought she did.

"We don't want you messing with his look anymore," Mr. Mathis told her. "We like the whole Oggie Cooder package — the clothes, the funny-looking dog, the weird noises, and especially those crazy shoelaces. And we think America is going to like it, too."

"Does that mean I can say 'yeppers' again, Mr. Mathis?" asked Oggie hopefully.

"Absolutely," said Mr. Mathis. "And forget the formality — we're a team now, Oggie. Please call me Brad."

"You know," said Mrs. Cooder, "now that I think of it, several kids came into the store yesterday, asking whether we had any seersucker pants. I wonder if that was because of Oggie."

Some of those kids were from Oggie's class, because over the next few days more and more of them showed up at Truman wearing things that had obviously come from the racks of Too Good to Be Threw.

The talk at Bethie Hudson's lunch table changed from horses to crocheting, and pretty soon all the girls were making homemade shoelaces just like Oggie's. Kids were getting into charving, too. Grocery stores in Wawatosa reported record sales of American cheese slices. The excitement about Oggie going to Hollywood was building to a fever pitch.

Donnica switched gears immediately and became as fierce about preserving Oggie's image as she had been about trying to change it.

"If any reporters show up, make sure you *prrr-rr-ip* as much as possible," she'd tell him. "And toss in a couple of yeppers, too."

She also suggested that besides saying "yeppers," he add "nopers" to his vocabulary.

Oggie didn't get it, but everybody who knew Donnica could tell that the reason she was helping Oggie was in order to get something for herself. And it worked, too. Once the papers got wind that Oggie's manager was a pretty little ten-year-old girl, they went nuts taking pictures of Donnica and Oggie together. *HT*, seeing the potential for even more publicity for the upcoming show, invited her to come with him to Hollywood. Donnica's ego immediately grew from large to jumbo size.

"Have you noticed she's calling people 'darling'?" Dawn said to Hannah one day at lunch.

"And now she's wearing sunglasses all the time, too," said Hannah. "The whole thing makes me sick."

Amy just shook her head.

Pretty soon, the papers started running stories about which contestants would prove to be the biggest competition for Oggie.

"You think Oggie can beat that guy with the stretchy nostrils?" Bethie Hudson asked one day.

"Of course he can beat him," said Donnica. "What's so great about being able to put quarters up your nose?"

"What about the girl who paints with pudding?" asked someone else.

"Who cares about pudding?" Donnica said, although truthfully the girl's remarkably accurate version of the *Mona Lisa* made entirely out of chocolate pudding had made her a little bit nervous.

"I've been thinking, maybe charving states isn't good enough," Donnica told Oggie one day at lunch. "What about presidents? You could charve Abe Lincoln with his top hat on. Or George Washington chopping down the cherry tree."

"That sounds kind of complicated," said Oggie.

"You want to win, don't you?" barked Donnica, pulling out her stopwatch. "Come on, Oggie Cooder. Give me George Washington and the cherry tree — and make it good!"

Oggie sighed and pulled a fresh piece of cheese out of his pocket. Charving sure was a lot less fun than it used to be.

On Friday, two days before Oggie and Donnica were supposed to fly to California to tape the show, Mr. Snolinovsky asked to see Oggie out in the hall.

"I'd better come, too," said Donnica. "I don't like my client to be interviewed when I'm not present."

"Donnica," Mr. Snolinovksy told her firmly, "go back to your seat, please. During school hours

Oggie is not your client, he is my student. And please don't make me say this again: *No sunglasses in my classroom.*"

Out in the hall, Mr. Snolinovsky leaned against the wall and scratched his head.

"Is there anything you'd like to talk about, Oggie?" he asked.

Oggie thought for a second. "Well," he said, "I have always kind of wondered why you scratch your head so much. When Turk is itchy, it usually means it's time for a flea bath."

Mr. Snolinovsky looked flustered. "I meant about the show," he said. "Are you sure it's not too much, all of this Hollywood hoo-ha?"

Oggie laughed. He liked that word "hoo-ha."

"I'm okay," he said. "My stomach feels kind of weird sometimes, though. I think it might be my appendix."

"It's more likely that you're nervous."

"The funny thing is," said Oggie, "I used to charve when I felt nervous. But ever since Donnica started timing me, and making me charve George Washington, it's not so relaxing anymore."

"Donnica can be a very persuasive girl," said Mr. Snolinovsky.

"Does persuasive mean the same thing as really bossy?" asked Oggie.

Mr. Snolinovsky laughed. "Just remember to be yourself, Oggie, and I'm sure you'll be fine."

At the end of the day, Mr. Snolinovsky dragged out his record player and the desks got pushed to the side of the room for square dancing. The first dance was a "ladies' choice" and all the girls made a beeline for Oggie. Everybody wanted to dance with the most famous fourth grader in Wawatosa, Wisconsin. That is, *almost* everybody. Amy stood in the corner watching Oggie and quietly shaking her head.

When Oggie and Donnica got home from school, Bradley Mathis's car was parked in the Cooders' driveway again. Mr. and Mrs. Cooder were down at the store, meeting with another plumber, so no one had been home to answer the doorbell, leaving Brad no choice but to wait on the porch steps.

"Oggie, we've got a problem," he said.

"Sorry, Brad, but before I do anything else I have to take Turk out," Oggie apologized. "Otherwise I might end up with the kind of problem that leaves a stain on the rug."

While Oggie walked Turk, Donnica sat down next to Brad on the steps and asked him what was the matter.

"The problem is, Oggie Fever is spreading faster than we thought it would. It's gone way beyond Wawatosa. Kids all over the country are starting to dress like him and act like him. They're saying 'yeppers.' And adopting shaggy dogs from the pound, crocheting shoelaces, and charving cheese. He's even got a fan club with a Web site — Prrrrrip.com."

"Isn't that a good thing?" asked Donnica, who would have given anything to have a fan club.

"You would think so," said Brad. "But the show won't air for another month after the taping, and the producers are worried that Oggie Cooder will be old news by that time. People won't care anymore."

Donnica felt her free ride to Hollywood slipping through her fingers.

"There has to be something we can do," she said, quickly jumping up. She pulled her lip gloss out of her pocket and began pacing nervously as she ran it over her lips. Suddenly, she stopped.

"I've got it!" Donnica said excitedly. "It's the exact same thing as the toaster! We have to turn up the dial!"

Brad looked confused. "On the toaster?" he asked.

"No, on Oggie. We have to turn up the dial on Oggie and make him *Oggier*," Donnica said.

A smile slowly spread across Brad's face.

"You know what?" he said. "I think you might be onto something here. Make Oggie *Oggier*, huh? I like it!"

19

n the time that it took Oggie to walk Turk around the block, Donnica and Brad had come up with a plan for how to make Oggie *Oggier*. Brad made several phone calls, then drove off in a hurry. Two minutes later, Donnica took off on her bicycle in the opposite direction.

"Where is everybody?" Oggie wondered aloud when he and Turk got back.

Thump! Thump! Thump!

Oggie heard a strange sound outside.

"Hey, Oggie!" someone called.

Oggie ran to the window and looked out. David Korben was standing in the driveway bouncing his basketball.

Thump! Thump! Thump!

"Hi, David," said Oggie as he came outside and stood on the porch. "What's up?"

"I just saw old bossy face ride off on her bicycle, so I figured maybe this would be a good time to come over and see if you want to play some B-ball."

"You mean now?" asked Oggie. "With you?"

"Sure, why not?" David said.

"I can't. I have to practice my charving. Donnica says my Ulysses S. Grant looks too much like Santa Claus."

"Oh, come on," said David. "The guys are all over at the courts by the school, waiting. We really want you to play with us."

"But Donnica says —"

"Who cares what she says?" interrupted David. "You can't spend all your time charving, can you? Besides, if you hang around with cheese too much, you might turn into a mouse, or something."

Oggie laughed.

"Well . . . maybe I could come play for a little while," he said.

His whole life Oggie had always been the last one picked when teams were being chosen for sports. But that day on the basketball court, David Korben won the coin toss, which meant he got first pick. He didn't even hesitate —

"I want Oggie."

Oggie grinned so hard his face hurt. And during the game, when he dribbled the ball out of bounds, or missed a basket, instead of laughing at him and calling him names, the boys gave him pointers.

"Step into it when you pass!"

"Bend your knees before you shoot!"

"Take your time, Cooder."

Oggie listened to everything they said, and he concentrated on playing basketball just the way he concentrated when he was charving cheese. Finally, it paid off and he made a basket! In fact, he made three.

"That was really fun," Oggie told the guys as they took turns at the drinking fountain after the game. "Thanks for helping me."

"No problem," said David, wiping his mouth with the back of his hand. "It's not every day we get to play with somebody famous like you."

Oggie blushed and grinned. Maybe this whole celebrity thing wasn't so bad. After all, he'd never been invited to play basketball before.

"Hey, Oggie," said one of the guys, "since you're the pro, how about you give us some charving lessons?"

"Sure," said Oggie.

"OVER MY DEAD BODY!"

Nobody had noticed Donnica's arrival. She'd been riding by the school on her way home and had noticed Oggie on the basketball court. She was furious.

"How dare you!" she shouted.

"What's the big deal, Donnica?" said David, "He was just playing a little B-ball. And you know something? He's not half bad."

Oggie started to *prrrrr-ip* from the compliment, but the look on Donnica's face stopped him cold.

"We're going," Donnica said, grabbing Oggie's arm and pulling him off the court. "Brad is probably already there waiting with the new cheese."

Oggie reluctantly waved good-bye to the guys. Donnica got back on her bike and told Oggie to run along beside her.

"How come Brad went to get more cheese?" Oggie asked, doing his best to keep up with Donnica. "I told you, my mom bought a whole bunch yesterday."

"That cheese is no good anymore," said Donnica. "We have to go bigger."

"Bigger?" said Oggie. He winced as his stomach pinched.

Donnica hit a bump in the road and put her hand out to steady the small cardboard box sitting in the basket attached to her handlebars.

"What's in there?" Oggie asked.

"That's for me to know and you to find out," Donnica answered mysteriously.

* * *

Brad was waiting on the steps when Oggie and Donnica arrived back at the Cooders' house.

"Did you get the cheese?" Donnica asked him.

Brad nodded.

"It's in the trunk. How about you? Did you find what you were looking for?"

Donnica carefully lifted the box out of her bike basket.

"It's perfect," she said. "Wait till you see."

Oggie opened the front door and let them in. Donnica carried the box inside and set it down on the floor. Oggie wasn't sure, but he thought he saw it move. Then he heard a strange whining sound. So did Turk, and the fur on the back of his neck stood up as he growled.

"What's in there?" Oggie asked again.

Donnica opened the box, reached in, and pulled out a small strange-looking creature with a pointy face like a rat and bumpy grayish-purple skin. The only fur on its body was a ratty pom-pom on the end of its tail and a tangle of white hair sprouting up from between its ears like a bad toupee.

"What *is* that?" gasped Oggie in horror.

"Oggie," said Donnica, scooping up the hideous creature and holding it out to him, "say hello to your new dog."

20

Turk barked, and the strange little dog pulled back her lips and showed him her teeth.

"What kind of a dog is that?" Oggie asked. "And why doesn't it have any fur?"

"It's called a Chinese Crested. I got it at The Pet Stop. Her name is Fuzzy."

"That's a pretty strange name for a bald dog," Oggie said.

Donnica turned to Brad.

"Didn't I tell you she was perfect?" she said.

"Like Turk, only Turkier." Brad laughed.

"What's that supposed to mean?" asked Oggie.

But instead of answering, Brad hurried outside, returning a minute later with a big wooden box.

Oggie took one side of the heavy box and helped carry it into the living room where they put it down on the coffee table.

"Phew, that sure is heavy. What's in there?"

"Cheese," Brad told him.

"Cheese?" said Oggie. "But it weighs a ton."

"Seventy-five pounds," said Brad.

"*You bought seventy-five pounds of cheese?*" Oggie couldn't believe it.

"Actually, I bought one hundred and fifty pounds. There's another box just like this one out in the car."

"Why do we need so much?" Oggie asked.

"Do you want to explain?" Brad asked Donnica.

"It's like cheese . . . only cheesier," Donnica said.

Oggie groaned and flopped down on the couch.

"Can somebody *please* tell me what's going on?" he said.

So Donnica and Brad explained to Oggie the studio's concerns about people burning out on "Oggie Fever."

"You don't want to be old news, do you?" Donnica said.

But before Oggie could tell her that he wouldn't mind being old news if it meant he could take a break from all the speed-charving she'd been making him do — the doorbell rang.

"That must be LaRue," said Brad.

"Who's LaRue?" asked Oggie.

Brad opened the door, and a tall woman in a gold jumpsuit and a turban breezed into the house.

She was holding several large garment bags and a Styrofoam head with a curly red wig on it.

"Which one is Oogie?" she purred, looking around the room.

"Uh, actually it's *Oggie*," Oggie told her. "With two *g*'s, not two *o*'s."

"LaRue is a costume designer I happen to know in the area," Brad explained. "She's been kind enough to agree to help us with your new look."

"New look?" said Oggie, "I thought you said I looked okay the way I was."

"That was before, this is now," said Donnica.

Turk, who normally loved having company in the house, was lying under the coffee table nervously looking up at Fuzzy, who was sitting on a throw pillow on the couch licking herself.

"I must see this *chooving* thing before I can pick the outfit," said LaRue.

"Do you mean charving?" asked Oggie.

LaRue pulled a tape measure out of the pocket of her jumpsuit and began to measure Oggie.

"Hush, Oogie," she said, pressing a long finger up to her lips. "No worries. LaRue will find something yummy for you."

While LaRue measured, Brad opened the wooden box, revealing a giant chunk of cheddar cheese.

"How am I supposed to charve that?" asked Oggie. "It's not even sliced."

"I told you," said Donnica, "no more slices. We're going bigger."

"Much bigger," said Brad. "Are you ready for this? You're going to be charving Mount Rushmore!"

"*Mount Rushmore?*" cried Oggie.

"It'll be easy," said Donnica. "You already know how to do all those presidents, remember?"

"I'm ready to see the chooving now," said LaRue, putting her tape measure away. "Show me the chooving, Oogie."

Oggie's head was spinning. Things were happening so fast.

"Ouch!" he exclaimed, as his stomach pinched sharply.

"Come on," said Donnica, pulling out her stop-watch, "we don't have much time left. You have to practice."

"I don't even remember what Mount Rushmore looks like!" Oggie protested.

"Don't worry," Brad told him, "I picked up a book about famous American landmarks. There's a picture of Mount Rushmore on page thirty-three."

"I don't know about this," said Oggie uncertainly, eyeing the huge piece of cheese sitting on the table in front of him.

"Trust me," said Donnica. Oggie's stomach pinched again.

As Oggie had suspected, *charving* Mount Rushmore turned out to be much more challenging than Donnica and Brad had made it out to be. For one thing, cheddar cheese had a different texture from American cheese. It was more apt to crumble, which was why Abraham Lincoln's nose and George Washington's eyebrows kept falling off.

Turk enjoyed gobbling up the scraps of cheese as they fell on the floor, but Oggie was miserable.

"Stop!" shouted LaRue, who had been perched on the arm of a chair nearby taking notes the whole time. "I see yellow!"

Oggie immediately looked at the rug to see if Turk had had an accident. But LaRue was talking about the clothes she wanted Oggie to wear.

"No more *chooving* now, Oogie. Time for LaRue to make you yummy."

Turk tried to join them as Oggie followed LaRue into the guest room. But LaRue pushed Turk away with her foot and closed the door in his face.

"I'm thinking knickers," LaRue said, unzipping one of her bags.

"Knickers?" said Oggie.

"Yummy yellow knickers," said LaRue.

Oggie had no idea what she was talking about.

"Can I still wear my shoelaces?" he asked. "They're pretty yummy, don't you think?"

LaRue looked at Oggie's feet and frowned.

"No," she said. "No, no no."

"What about striped pants?" asked Oggie. "Or maybe a checkered shirt? I'd be comfortable in those."

But Oggie's "new look" was not going to have stripes or checks. It was going to have yummy yellow knickers. As the final pieces of the let's-make-Oggie-Oggier plan fell into place, Oggie's stomach pinched harder and he wondered how much more he could take.

21

While Oggie was busy getting his fashion makeover, Brad went out to the car to bring in the other box of cheese.

"Why are there so many reporters outside?" Brad asked, a few minutes later as he came in carrying the heavy box.

Donnica knew why they were there. Without telling anyone, she had called a press conference to stir up some excitement.

"I'll take care of them," she said, quickly pulling out her lip gloss and applying a fresh coat before heading outside to face the cameras.

Donnica loved dealing with the press. As they crowded around her with their cameras and notepads ready, she informed them that her "client" was involved in some top-secret last-minute pre-parations for the show and would not be available to speak with them. But they were more than wel-come to take as many pictures of *her* as they wanted.

Back inside, LaRue and Brad were sitting on the couch with Fuzzy between them, waiting for Oggie to come out and model the outfit LaRue had cho-sen for him to wear on the show.

"What's taking so long, Oogie?" LaRue called impatiently. "Do you need help with the zippers?"

"No!" shouted Oggie, who had absolutely insisted that he did not want LaRue in the room with him while he was getting dressed. "I'll be out in a minute."

When Oggie finally did emerge, his face was so red it looked like he had a sunburn.

"I don't know about this outfit," Oggie said uncertainly. He peeked around the corner before shuffling uncomfortably out into the living room. He had on a pair of bright yellow pants that only came down to his knees, a shirt with giant buttons

and extremely puffy sleeves, and on his feet, a pair of wooden clogs like the kind Dutch people wear. The curly red wig was in his hand.

"Don't you have any pants that go all the way down?" he asked.

"Knickers are more yummy for you," said LaRue with a dismissive wave of her hand. "Put on the wig."

"It's itchy," Oggie complained.

Unconcerned with his discomfort, LaRue came over and put the wig on Oggie's head.

"It does kind of work, Oogie, I mean, Oggie," said Brad.

Oggie gasped as the worst stomach cramp so far hit him. He folded over in pain, and that's when he noticed the back door was ajar.

"Where's Turk?" he asked anxiously.

"The big dog?" LaRue responded. "With all the hair?"

"Yes," Oggie told her. "Where is the big dog?"

"He let it out," LaRue said with a little wave toward Brad.

"*What?*" cried Oggie.

"I turned my back for two seconds and he ate half of Mount Rushmore," Brad explained, "so I put him outside. I figured it was okay, since the yard is fenced in."

But what Brad didn't know was that the latch on the gate was broken. When Oggie ran out into the backyard, he found that the worst possible thing had happened.

Turk was gone!

22

Oggie kicked off the heavy wooden shoes, jammed his feet into his sneakers, and took off.

"What are you doing?" Donnica screamed when Oggie burst out the door. "Don't let them see you! You'll ruin everything!"

The minute the reporters caught sight of Oggie, of course the cameras started clicking furiously. And they followed him as he ran up the street, whistling and frantically calling Turk's name.

Finally, Oggie caught sight of Turk, scratching under the big bush on the corner. He'd gone to retrieve the tennis ball he'd left there the other day.

"There you are," said Oggie, relieved. But when he reached out to grab hold of Turk's collar, the dog growled at him.

Oggie was stunned. Turk had never growled at him before. Ever. He only did that to strangers or people he didn't trust.

"What's the matter, Turkey?" cried Oggie in dismay. "Don't you like me anymore?"

Hot and sweaty from running, Oggie reached up to scratch his head and suddenly he understood. No wonder Turk had growled at him — he didn't recognize him!

"Okay, okay, I get the message, boy," Oggie said. He yanked off the red wig and threw it on the ground. Then he ripped off the ridiculous shirt, sending several of the big buttons flying. He would have taken off those silly yellow pants, too, except the photographers had caught up with him and he didn't want them taking pictures of him in his underwear. Brad was there by now, and so was LaRue, with the hideous Fuzzy under her arm. Turk, no longer confused, was barking and jumping up on Oggie to lick his face. But the happy reunion between boy and dog did not last long.

"Do you have any idea what you've done?" Donnica

shouted as she pushed her way through the crowd. "I told you not to let them see you. You've ruined all our hard work. What's the matter with you? Don't you want to go to Hollywood? Don't you want to be the most famous fourth grader in the world? What is your problem, Oggie Cooder? *DON'T YOU WANT TO WIN?*"

Oggie felt a monster stomach cramp beginning to rise up inside of him.

The crowd grew silent as they waited for him to respond. And in the quiet, Oggie finally found the answer to the question Donnica had asked him so many times.

"No, Donnica," he said, shaking his head. "I don't want to win. *You* do."

Donnica's eyes were ablaze.

"That's right," she snarled through gritted teeth. "And we made a deal, Oggie Cooder. I'm your manager, and I say that we are going to Hollywood together whether you like it or not. Now pick up your hair and get moving."

Oggie didn't move.

"I said, *PICK UP YOUR HAIR*," Donnica commanded, pointing at the red wig lying on the sidewalk.

Oggie took a deep breath.

"First of all," he said, "that is *not* my hair. And second of all, I don't want to charve Mount Rushmore. And third of all, that bald rat over there is not my dog. And fourth of all, these are definitely *not* my pants."

Oggie stopped to catch his breath.

"Are you finished?" snapped Donnica.

"Not quite," Oggie told her. And that's when Mr. Snolinovsky's words came back to him. Not the ones about how important it was to be yourself — he'd figured that part out when his own dog hadn't been able to recognize him. It was the other thing he'd said that Oggie felt was just right for this occasion. "Fifth of all," he said to Donnica, "I've had enough of this Hollywood hoo-ha."

As the reporters scribbled notes for their final Oggie Cooder stories, Turk barked happily, then grabbed his tennis ball.

For the first time in days, Oggie's stomach didn't ache. He actually felt happy, from the top of his head right down to the tips of his crocheted shoelaces.

"Come on, boy," Oggie said to Turk. "Let's go home."

23

After saying good-bye to *Hidden Talents*, Oggie Cooder's life went back to normal . . . even if it was a different kind of normal than before. Everybody in town knew who he was now, but nobody wanted to write newspaper articles about him anymore. Sales of American cheese slices leveled off, and kids went back to wearing regular shoelaces. David Korben and his buddies were shocked at first when they heard that Oggie had given up a chance to be on TV. But they decided it was pretty cool the way he'd stood up to Donnica Perfecto, and Oggie was invited to become a regular player at their after-school basketball games.

Dawn Perchy and Hannah Hummerman eventually forgave Donnica for what she'd done. They went back to eating lunch together at the table by the window, although Dawn and Hannah absolutely refused to finish her words for her anymore. And as for Donnica Perfecto, she held tight to her grudge against Oggie Cooder, vowing that someday she would get him back for ruining her plans to go to Hollywood. Especially when, in a rare showing of parental backbone, Mrs. Perfecto handed her daughter a spatula and insisted that she scrape the cheese off her ceiling.

Oggie was as happy as a clam. The only thing he regretted about deciding not to go on *Hidden Talents* was that he had planned to give the ten thousand dollars to his parents to pay for new pipes. The cost of the pipes became less of an issue, though, when a collector who'd read about the Cooders' store in one of the many newspaper articles written about Oggie stopped in and bought that old Howdy Doody hat for a very large sum of money.

Mr. Snolinovsky gave Oggie an A on his story about Turk and the licorice. He also wrote some very nice things about Oggie on his report card, including this: *"Oggie's positive attitude and his good self-esteem make him an excellent role model for his classmates."* Mrs. Cooder beamed proudly as she glued the report card into the family scrapbook.

One Friday afternoon, Mr. Snolinovsky's fourth graders pushed their desks to the side of the room and got ready to square-dance. The first dance was a "ladies choice," and Amy Schneider chose Oggie to be her partner.

"So, are you coming over, Oggie?" she asked as they hooked elbows and began to swing each other around. "My mom said she would make us popcorn and root beer floats if we want."

The final episode of *Hidden Talents* was going to be on that night, and since Amy knew that Oggie didn't have a TV at home, she had invited him to come over and watch it at her house.

"What time did you say it starts?" asked Oggie.

Amy was about to answer when Oggie tripped on one of his shoelaces and accidentally stepped on her foot.

"Ouch!" cried Amy, but then she giggled and told him to be there at eight o' clock.

The girl who painted with pudding ended up winning the grand prize on *Hidden Talents* that night. As Oggie sat on Amy Schneider's couch happily munching popcorn and watching the television audience go nuts, clapping and cheering, he couldn't contain himself, either.

"*Prrrrr-ip! Prrrrr-ip!*" went Oggie. Because even though it wasn't him up there on that Hollywood stage, Oggie Cooder finally knew what it felt like to be a winner, and he thought it was just about the best feeling in the world.

Oggie Cooder

PARTY
ANIMAL!

For Pat Fedler and her beautiful New
granddaughter, Madison

1

Prrrrr-ip! Prrrrr-ip!

Oggie Cooder fluttered his tongue against the roof of his mouth. He always did that when he was excited about something.

"Check it out, Turk," he cried happily. "Look who just got invited to Donnica Perfecto's birthday party. *Can you believe it?*"

Oggie's dog, Turk, loved to eat paper. So when Oggie proudly held out the invitation he'd just received in the morning mail, Turk misunderstood and thought he was being offered a snack. In two quick bites the invitation disappeared.

"Hey!" Oggie laughed. "You were supposed to *read* it, not *eat* it!"

Turk, whose full name was Turkey-on-Rye (like the sandwich), burped and wagged his tail.

Oggie finished eating his breakfast and carried his empty cereal bowl over to the sink to rinse it out. Looking out the window, he saw Donnica Perfecto coming out of her house, her bubblegum-pink backpack slung over one shoulder. Mrs. Perfecto, in a long flowered bathrobe and hair curlers, followed after her daughter. She looked nervous.

"Don't worry, Cupcake!" she called. "Everything's going to be fine on Saturday. *Just fine.*" Then she blew a kiss and waved, but Donnica only glared at her and marched off.

Grabbing his own backpack, Oggie made a quick pit stop at the fridge for a few slices of processed American cheese, which he slipped into his back pocket for later. He gave Turk a good-bye pat on the head and raced out the door.

"Hey, Donnica! Wait up!" Oggie cried as he ran down the front steps.

Ever since his aunt Hettie had taught him how to crochet, Oggie had been making his own shoelaces. The night before, he'd crocheted himself a new pairing — orange and green, one of his favorite color combinations. Oggie thought they went nicely with the new blue-and-yellow-checked pants his mother had brought home from the store for him that week. Unfortunately one of the shoelaces was a little too long, and when the end of it caught on a loose nail on the steps, Oggie went tumbling head over heels into the bushes. Luckily he wasn't hurt, but by the time he pulled himself together, brushed the leaves out of his hair, and retied his shoelace in a double bow, Donnica had rounded the corner and was out of sight.

Oggie finally caught up with her in the schoolyard at Truman Elementary.

"I hope you don't mind," Oggie panted, holding his side and trying to catch his breath, "but I have about a *bazillion* questions I need to ask you."

"What's the matter with you, Oggie Cooder?" Donnica snarled as she spun around on her heel to face him. "Can't you see I'm having the worst day of my life?"

Now that she mentioned it, Oggie did notice that Donnica's eyebrows were scrunched down and bunched together in a knot over the top of her pointy little nose. And her shiny pink gloss-covered lips, which were usually turned up in a self-satisfied smirk, were pulled down at the corners in an unhappy pout.

Oggie hated to see people upset. Even Donnica Perfecto, who wasn't very nice to him.

"What's wrong?" he asked with genuine concern.

"You mean besides the fact that those pants you've got on are so hideous they're giving me a headache?" Donnica said.

"Maybe you should ask the school nurse for an aspirin," said Oggie. He didn't realize that Donnica's head wasn't really hurting, she was just making fun of his pants.

"Aspirin isn't going to fix what's wrong with my life," Donnica complained.

"What's wrong with your life?" Oggie asked,

surprised. It seemed to him Donnica Perfecto had a pretty great life. For one thing, she had a swimming pool in her backyard. When Oggie felt hot, the only way he had to cool off was to run through the sprinkler.

"I'll tell you what's wrong with my life," Donnica grumbled. "Because of my father and his stupid, boring old store, my whole birthday party is ruined."

Mr. Perfecto owned the largest appliance store in Wawatosa, Wisconsin. Walk into any house in town, chances were that the microwave in the kitchen and the television in the den had been purchased from Big Dealz. Any house, that is, except Oggie's. Mr. and Mrs. Cooder believed that microwave ovens and televisions — not to mention marshmallows, air fresheners, and milk sold in plastic jugs — were all bad for your brain cells.

"Are you planning to have your party at your dad's store?" asked Oggie, who hadn't had time to study the details of the invitation before Turk had eaten it.

Donnica heaved an exasperated sigh.

"Why would anybody have a birthday party in an appliance store?" she asked.

"I don't know." Oggie shrugged. "If I had a swimming pool like yours, I'd have my birthday party there."

The Perfectos lived directly across Tullahoma Street from the Cooders, and although Oggie had never been in their beautiful sky-blue kidney-shaped swimming pool, Turk had jumped in once, uninvited, after managing to get loose one day.

"*Obviously*, I'm going to have a pool party," said Donnica. "I *always* have a pool party. But I already told everybody that this year was going to be different. I told them there would be a big surprise. Who's going to want to come to a plain old ordinary pool party now?"

"I will!" cried Oggie, who had never been invited to any of Donnica's parties before.

Oggie undid the strings on his backpack and pulled out a plastic bag filled with dried apricots.

"Want one?" he asked Donnica.

"Ewww," she said, turning up her nose at the apricots. "They're *brown*."

"That's 'cause they're from the health food store. My mom says the orange ones you get at the grocery store have a ton of chemicals in them that can ruin your brain cells."

Donnica ignored him and went back to her whining.

"It's just not fair," she said. "Why does Daddy's big promotion for his store have to be on the same day as my party? Why didn't he listen to me when I told him what I wanted? It's my birthday. I'm supposed to get everything I want for my birthday. That's the rule."

This seemed like the perfect opportunity for Oggie to ask Donnica the most important of the *bazillion* questions he had for her.

"What do you want for your birthday?" he said.

"I want to get you something that you'll really, really like because I'm really, really happy that you invited me to your party. Actually, I'm not really, really happy. *Prrrrr-ip! Prrrrr-ip!* I'm more like really, really, *really* —"

"I get the point," Donnica interrupted. Oggie Cooder was more annoying than a broken fingernail.

The big red doors of Truman Elementary School swung open and students began filing into the building to begin the day.

"So anyway," said Oggie, trotting along next to Donnica as they started up the steps of the school, "can you think of something I could give you for your birthday?"

Donnica was about to tell Oggie to get lost and quit bothering her, when a lightbulb suddenly went on over her head. Actually there *was* something she wanted Oggie to give her for her birthday! Something Donnica had been wanting from the moment Mrs. Perfecto had made her write Oggie's name on one of her bubblegum-pink party invitations. Donnica wanted Oggie Cooder NOT to come to her party. And as anyone who knew her would tell you, Donnica Perfecto was really good at getting what she wanted.

Really, really, *really* good.

2

Oggie didn't have time to think about Donnica's birthday party anymore that morning. He had to work on a history report, which was due the following week. The topic he'd chosen for his report was famous inventors, which was no big surprise since Inventor was among the top ten things Oggie thought he might like to be when he grew up.

In the library, Oggie found a book called *Whose Idea Was It?* that looked promising. He sat down, opened it up to the table of contents, and began to run his finger down a list of famous inventors.

Alexander Graham Bell
George Washington Carver
Thomas Edison
Henry Ford

Benjamin Franklin
Samuel Morse
Elisha Otis

Oggie stopped.

"Who's Elisha Otis?" he wondered aloud. He flipped through the pages until he found the chapter describing how, in 1854, Elisha Otis had demonstrated the new elevator he had invented by ascending to a dizzying height in front of a crowd of people at a state fair and then having his assistant cut the ropes to prove that the brakes he had fashioned out of two wagon springs would keep the elevator from plummeting to the ground.

"*Prrrrr-ip! Prrrrr-ip!*" Oggie found that very exciting.

Donnica, who was sitting at a nearby table, gave Oggie a dirty look.

"Must you make that annoying sound?" she whined.

"I can't help it," Oggie told her excitedly. "I never knew who invented elevator brakes before."

"Shhh," said Ms. Hepper, the school librarian, pressing a long pale finger to her lips. "Do I need to remind you that the library is a quiet place, Oggie?"

"Sorry," Oggie whispered apologetically.

As Oggie turned the pages of the book, he was fascinated to learn about all kinds of interesting and important things people had invented over the years. Steam engines and telegraphs, ice-cream makers and electronic cow-milkers. The more he read, the more convinced he became that being an inventor would be a great profession for him. He hoped he could be like Elisha Otis and invent something as useful as elevator brakes.

At 11:45, Ms. Hepper announced to the students in the library that they had ten minutes left to finish up. Oggie carried his book over to the circulation desk to check it out.

"Necessity is the mother of invention," whispered Ms. Hepper with an approving nod as she ran the scanner over Oggie's book.

"Excuse me?" said Oggie.

"I believe it was Plato who said it," she told him.

Oggie had never heard of the great philosopher Plato. In fact, he'd misunderstood Ms. Hepper completely and thought that she had said "Plano," which was a town in Texas Oggie knew about because his uncle Vern had once ridden on a pig in a rodeo competition there.

"It means that the main reason things get invented is because people feel a need to have them," Ms. Hepper explained.

Oggie thought about that for a second and decided it made a lot of sense, though he wasn't sure what it had to do with Plano, Texas.

When he got back to his classroom, Oggie stashed his library book in his desk, grabbed his lunch, and headed down to the cafeteria, or — as some of the kids at Truman liked to call it — the *Barf-eteria*. Amy Schneider was waiting for Oggie when he got there.

"Who invented braces?" Oggie asked as he plopped himself down in his usual spot across the table from Amy.

Amy and Oggie were friends. Not boyfriend and girlfriend, just friends who happened to be a boy and a girl. Amy didn't mind that Oggie said *prrrrr-ip!* when he was excited about something, and Oggie didn't mind that Amy was shy and had a mouth so full of braces and rubber bands that it was sometimes hard to understand her when she spoke. Amy had to remove her rubber bands whenever she ate, and she was just finishing up the process when Oggie arrived.

"I don't know who invented braces," she said, dropping the last of the tiny green rubber bands onto the neat little pile she had made on her napkin. "But whoever it was must be rich. My parents told me that with all the money they've spent on straightening my teeth, they could have bought a brand-new car."

"I bet you could *make* a car out of all that metal in your mouth," said Oggie. "And you could use the rubber bands to make the tires."

Amy giggled and took a nice, big, rubber-band-free bite of her tuna fish sandwich.

Meanwhile, across the cafeteria at a round table in a prime spot near the window, Donnica Perfecto was about to deliver the bad news to her friends, Dawn and Hannah.

"My birthday party is going to be a disaster," she said. "And I'm talking a *total* disaster."

"I thought you told us there was going to be a big surprise," said Dawn.

"Yeah, remember you said it was going to be the biggest surprise ever?" Hannah reminded her.

"Well, it's not happening," Donnica reported.

"But you've been talking about it for weeks!" Hannah pressed. "You said this was going to be your best —"

"I know what I said," snapped Donnica. "But it's not happening. Read my lips: TOTAL DISASTER. Got it?"

"At least tell us what the surprise was going to be," Hannah said.

"Trust me. You don't want to know," Donnica replied as she pulled the lid off her Peachy-Keen-O-flavored yogurt, licked it, and then handed it to Hannah, who took it from her without a word.

Donnica Perfecto didn't "do" garbage. When she had something that needed to be thrown out, she simply handed it to Hannah or Dawn and they took care of it for her. Hannah took the sticky yogurt lid and placed it next to her own banana peel and crumpled napkin.

"Come on," Dawn begged. "Tell us what the surprise was going to be."

Donnica took a bite of yogurt, then set her spoon down.

"Okay," she finally agreed, "but don't say I didn't warn you. You're going to be totally bummed out when I tell you who was *almost* going to be the entertainment at my party."

Dawn and Hannah looked at Donnica expectantly.

"Tell us already," Hannah urged.

Donnica took a deep breath before answering — *"Cheddar Jam."*

3

Dawn and Hannah were so stunned their mouths fell open in simultaneous shock.

"*Cheddar Jam?*" Hannah managed to croak.

"Are you saying what I think you're saying?" Dawn gasped in amazement. "Were they really going to play at your party?"

Donnica groaned and covered her face with both hands.

Cheddar Jam (a rock band named in honor of one of Wisconsin's most important contributions to the world — cheddar cheese) was made up of four *very* cute and *somewhat* musical local high school boys. They'd made quite a splash at Truman Elementary when they'd played at the Valentine Dance earlier that year.

"I told you you'd be bummed out," said Donnica.

"That's the understatement of the century," Hannah told her.

"Why aren't they coming?" Dawn asked.

"Because Daddy totally blew it," Donnica said bitterly. "He told me he was going to get somebody good to entertain at the store in the morning and then pay them extra to come over to my party afterward. So I told him to get Cheddar Jam. That's what I said — '*Daddy, get me Cheddar Jam*' — but did he listen?"

Donnica heaved a heavy sigh and picked up her spoon to take a bite of yogurt, but she changed her mind and pushed the plastic container toward Hannah, who added it to the throwaway pile. The girls were quiet for a minute and then Dawn asked —

"If Cheddar Jam isn't coming, who did your dad get instead?"

Donnica could barely bring herself to answer.

"Bumbles," she muttered through clenched teeth.

"*What?*" cried Hannah in disbelief.

"No way!" said Dawn.

"It's not my fault," Donnica said defensively. "I *told* my father to get Cheddar Jam. I can't help it if he got Bumbles the Juggling Bear instead."

"Why don't you do what you did when you wanted a new cell phone?" Dawn suggested.

"Yeah," said Hannah. "Pitch a fit and tell him if he doesn't give you what you want, you're not going to let him walk you down the aisle on your wedding day."

"Uh, *duh*. Don't you think I tried that already? He said it was too late. He already promised Bumbles the job. He said Bumbles told him he's broke and needs the work." Donnica groaned and put her head in her hands again.

Over on the other side of the room, Oggie Cooder had somehow managed to spill an entire carton of chocolate milk on the floor. He'd tried to use his sandwich as a sponge to soak up the milk, but that had only made matters worse. On his way over to the lunch counter to get some paper napkins to clean up the mess, he passed near Donnica's table and figured he'd take the opportunity to ask another of his *bazillion* important questions about her birthday party.

"Hey, Donnica?" he called to her. "Is it okay if I wear my bathing suit over to your house on Saturday, or should I bring it with me and change into it when I get there?"

For the second time that day, Dawn's and Hannah's mouths dropped open in simultaneous shock. Had Donnica actually invited *Oggie Cooder* to her birthday party?

"I know what you're thinking," Donnica told them. "But it wasn't *my* idea."

It was Donnica's mother who had insisted that Oggie be invited to the party.

"I want you to send an invitation to the Cooder boy across the street," Mrs. Perfecto had announced one morning as Donnica sat at the table carefully addressing the envelopes for her party invitations.

"You must be joking, Mother. Why would I do that?" asked Donnica.

"He's our neighbor, Cupcake."

"So what? He plays with cheese and makes that annoying sound with his tongue all the time. Plus he dresses like he's from another planet. Yesterday he wore a bow tie to school. *A bow tie*, Mother."

"I admit he's a bit odd," Mrs. Perfecto had said. "But the Wawatosa Gardening Club is considering me for membership."

"So?" said Donnica, running the tip of her pointy tongue along an envelope flap before adding it to the pile to be stamped.

"I've wanted to be in that club for years. Everyone who's anyone is in it," Mrs. Perfecto explained.

"Why don't you just join if you want to be in it so badly?"

"It's not that easy. You have to be invited. The board of directors comes and examines your landscaping before they'll even consider you for membership."

"What's landscaping?" asked Donnica, licking another flap and tossing the envelope onto the pile.

"Flowers and bushes," said Mrs. Perfecto.

"We have plenty of flowers and bushes," Donnica pointed out.

"Yes, but they're all droopy and sad-looking," said Mrs. Perfecto. "That is, they were until Isabel Cooder stepped in. Ever since she showed me how to put crushed eggshells around my plants to keep away the slugs, my begonias have been blooming like there's no tomorrow."

"Hello? What do eggshells have to do with inviting Oggie Cooder to my birthday party?" Donnica asked.

"I need to stay on Isabel Cooder's good side. She's my only hope of getting into the club."

"*Mother*," Donnica whined, "Oggie Cooder is the dweebiest dweeb to ever walk the earth. I'll *die* of embarrassment if he comes to my birthday party."

But Mrs. Perfecto's mind was made up. She stood over Donnica as she wrote Oggie's name on one of the pink envelopes. Then, to make sure that Donnica didn't "accidentally" forget to mail it, Mrs. Perfecto carried the invitation down to the corner and dropped it into the mailbox herself.

If Mrs. Perfecto thought that the battle was over and she had won, then clearly she had forgotten who she was dealing with.

"You're joking, right?" said Hannah. "You didn't really invite Oggie Cooder to your party, did you?"

Donnica reached into her pocket and pulled out her pink lip gloss.

"I invited him," she said, pausing for a minute to slowly run the shiny gloss over her lips. "But trust me, he's not going to come."

4

Lunch hour was over. Hannah took care of throwing out the trash, then she and Dawn took up their usual positions on either side of Donnica, and the trio exited the Barf-eteria together. Amy Schneider and Oggie Cooder were in the same fourth-grade class as Donnica Perfecto and her friends, so they headed down the hall in the same direction toward Mr. Snolinovsky's classroom. At the beginning of the year Oggie had found it difficult to remember how to pronounce his teacher's name correctly. *SNOW-LINN-OFF-SKEE* was much harder to say than the names of any of his other teachers had been.

That afternoon in class, Oggie couldn't seem

to stop *prrrrr-ip-ing*. Mr. Snolinovsky spoke to him about it several times, but even so, Oggie *prr-rrr-ip-ed* in the middle of math and twice during science. He was so excited about having been invited to Donnica's birthday party he simply couldn't contain himself. Oggie had always wondered what it would be like to swim in the Perfectos' pool, and now at last he was going to find out.

The last hour of every school day, Mr. Snolinovsky's class did creative writing. At the beginning of the year, Oggie had worried that he wouldn't be able to think of anything interesting to write about. But once Mr. Snolinovsky had explained to him that stories were like seeds, and that Oggie was like a watermelon, loaded with seeds, Creative Writing had become his favorite subject. During the hour, Mr. Snolinovsky liked to walk around the room, peering over people's shoulders to see what they were working on.

"Fascinating," he said that day as he looked at the story Bethie Hudson was writing about her goldfish, Honeymoon.

"Exciting," he said as he read the paragraph David Korben had just finished about a slam-dunk contest he'd been in at basketball camp.

"Hmmm," he said as he bent down and squinted hard at Oggie's paper. "Does that sentence say 'Uncle Worm was from Switzerland'?"

Oggie had terrible handwriting, so it was no surprise that Mr. Snolinovsky was having trouble reading what he had written.

"No. It says, 'Uncle Vern won the Stinkerama,'" Oggie explained. "It's an armpit contest they have every year at the Zanesville County Fair. My uncle is the champion. He can play 'Yankee Doodle' with his hand under his arm, *and* his pits have been voted the stinkiest in the county for three years straight."

"Impressive," said Mr. Snolinovsky, stroking his mustache.

"That's nothing," Oggie told him. "You should see Uncle Vern chunk a mini-pumpkin. He made this catapult thing out of some old underwear elastic and a pair of chopsticks and, man oh man, he can make those babies fly. They have a contest for that in Zanesville, too."

Mr. Snolinovsky laughed. His name might have been difficult to pronounce, but he was the first teacher Oggie had ever had who not only accepted Oggie for who he was, but seemed to genuinely like him.

When Creative Writing was over, everybody put their stories away and Mr. Snolinovsky wrote the homework assignment for that night on the board. There was a page of math problems to solve in the workbook, a spelling test to prepare for, and, at the bottom of the list, a strange word Oggie had never seen before — *HAIKU*.

"What's *hay-cue*?" asked America Johnson, leaning forward in her seat as she squinted at the blackboard.

"It's pronounced *high-coo*, and it's a kind of Japanese poem," Mr. Snolinovsky explained.

There was an unhappy grumble from the class, especially the boys.

"Poetry stinks," groaned Jackson Polito.

"I'm down with that," agreed David Korben, who was interested in only one thing in life — basketball.

"You like math, don't you, Jackson?" Mr. Snolinovsky asked.

"Sure. Math is about numbers. Numbers are cool. Poetry is about mushy feelings and butterflies and other *un*-cool junk like that," Jackson said.

"What would you say if I told you that haiku is a kind of poetry that uses numbers?" asked Mr. Snolinovsky.

"Poems about numbers?" said Dylan James, who hardly ever talked in class. Dylan had thick, blond hair, which he had a habit of smoothing back with both hands. Oggie had heard that his family had moved to Wawatosa from Chicago over the summer.

Bethie Hudson waved her hand in the air excitedly.

"Listen to what I just made up!" she said when Mr. Snolinovsky called on her. "'Roses are red, violets are blue, two times eleven is twenty-two.'"

Mr. Snolinovsky smiled.

"Very nice," he said. "And I'm delighted to see you've been working on your times tables, Bethie. But when you write haiku, the only numbers you have to be concerned with are five, seven, and five."

"Don't tell me you're going to make us write five hundred and seventy-five words!" Jackson cried in horror.

"Don't worry," said Mr. Snolinovsky. "A haiku is a very short poem. It doesn't rhyme and it's only three lines long."

"Yes!" cried Jackson.

"So what do the two fives and the seven have to do with anything?" asked America.

"You use those numbers to count the syllables in your poem," Mr. Snolinovsky explained.

"You mean the poem only has to have sixteen syllables?" asked David, whose strongest subject was obviously not math.

"Seventeen," corrected Mr. Snolinovsky. "And, yes, that's how many syllables the poem has to have.

Five in the first line, seven in the second, and five in the third line."

"Do the words have to be in Japanese?" asked Donnica. "Because the only Japanese word I know is 'sushi,' and I am *not* writing a poem about raw fish."

Mr. Snolinovsky assured everyone that he did not expect the poems to be written in Japanese. Then he read a few examples from a book of haiku. The one that Oggie liked best was about a dog waiting for its owner to return home.

Friend beside the door
Ears up, head cocked, he listens
Eager for footsteps

Turk was always very happy to see Oggie when he got home. And he was usually waiting right at the door when Oggie got there. Oggie wondered whether that was because Turk was listening for his footsteps like the dog in the poem.

"I want each of you to write a haiku tonight and bring it in to class tomorrow," said Mr. Snolinovsky. "We're going to do something with them that I think you'll find very interesting,"

Actually, most of the kids in the class would find it interesting. But for one person — a certain individual sitting in the first seat of the third row in Mr. Snolinovsky's fourth grade classroom — the experience was going to be absolutely *shocking*.

5

Amy raised her hand.

"What are our haikus supposed to be about?" she asked.

"Before I answer that, Amy, let me point out that the plural of 'haiku' is 'haiku,' not 'haikus,'" said Mr. Snolinovsky. "And I want the haiku to be about you."

"Gross, we gotta write a poem about *Amy*? What if we don't want to write about *a girl*?" moaned Jonathan Bass, who had five sisters at home, which was five too many as far as he was concerned.

Mr. Snolinovsky laughed. "What I meant, Jon, is that I want each of you to write a haiku that tells us who you are."

216

Jackson was counting on his fingers.

"Awesome!" he shouted. "I've got my first and last lines already: *Jackson Polito*. Pretty lucky to have a name with five syllables, huh?"

"Mine, too!" cried Hannah Hummerman excitedly.

"Hang on," said Mr. Snolinovsky. "In order for us to do what I have in mind, you may not use your names in your haiku."

"No fair!" cried Jackson.

"Yeah," agreed David Korben, who hadn't counted carefully enough and thought that his name had five syllables, too.

"In addition to keeping your names out of the poems, I also don't want you to put your names on your papers," Mr. Snolinovsky went on.

"How are you going to know whose is whose?" asked America.

"That's where the challenge lies. If your haiku contains the *essence* of who you are, then it should be obvious who wrote it."

"What do you mean by 'essence'?" David asked.

"I think it has something to do with shampoo," Dawn said.

"I thought 'essence' meant something smelly," said Jonathan.

"Like Uncle Vern's armpits, you mean?" Oggie asked.

Donnica rolled her eyes. Oggie Cooder was *so* annoying. If he wasn't *prrrrr-ip-ing* all over the place or wearing bow ties, he was talking about his strange relatives in Ohio. There was no way, NO WAY he was coming to her birthday party. She was definitely going to see to that.

"Jonathan is right — 'essence' can mean smelly in some instances," Mr. Snolinovsky explained to the class, "but in this case it means something else." He pulled one of the classroom dictionaries off the shelf, turned to *E*, and read the definition: "Essence: the choicest or most important part of an idea, experience, or person." He slid the dictionary back into its place on the shelf and turned to the class. "I want your haiku to be about the choicest, most important part of what makes you who you are."

A few minutes later, as the class lined up at the door for dismissal, Donnica wasn't thinking about the essence of who she was. Instead, she was demonstrating it.

"How could Daddy possibly think that I would want a juggling bear at my party?" she whined to her friends. "Juggling bears are for babies. Do I look like a baby? I mean, *really*. A juggling bear? Puh —"

"— leeze." Dawn and Hannah automatically finished Donnica's word for her.

Following an argument they'd had with Donnica earlier in the year, Dawn and Hannah had threatened to stop finishing her words for her. But the habit had proved too difficult to break.

As they left the classroom and started down the hall, Oggie and Amy, who were walking next to each other, got close enough to be able to overhear the tail end of what Donnica was saying.

"How could this be happening to me?" she said. "Bumbles the Bear at *my* birthday party."

As soon as Oggie heard that, he let loose a particularly enthusiastic *prrrrr-ip!*

Donnica cringed at the sound.

Oggie had seen Bumbles many times, juggling at the farmers' market on Sunday mornings. Bumbles wasn't a real bear — he was a person dressed up in a fur suit who juggled bowling pins and fruit and other assorted objects in hopes that the people who stopped to watch would toss coins or, better yet, dollar bills into the battered black top hat he set out on the sidewalk. Oggie loved to watch Bumbles. He was funny and even though he sometimes pretended to drop things, that was just part of the act. He was actually a very good juggler.

"*Prrrrr-ip! Prrrrr-ip!* First you invite me to your party, and now I find out that Bumbles is going to be there, too?! I can't believe it!" Oggie exclaimed happily.

"Me neither," grumbled Donnica.

Everybody was so busy thinking about Donnica's birthday party that nobody was paying any attention to Amy Schneider. If they had been, they would have noticed that she suddenly looked terribly uncomfortable.

"I'll see you tomorrow," she told Oggie, then hurried off down the hall.

Oggie stopped to get a drink of water at the drinking fountain while Donnica and her friends continued walking.

"Do you realize this could ruin my reputation?" Donnica said glumly.

Dawn shot a quick look at Hannah. Donnica was their friend, but her reputation wasn't exactly something to be proud of, unless you happened to think that being bossy, mean, and completely self-centered was a *good* thing.

"Just think, if Cheddar Jam had come to your party, I would have gotten to meet J.J. in person." Hannah sighed. "Maybe he would have even come over and talked to me. I one-hundred-percent guarantee that if that ever happened I would totally faint from happiness." She put the back of her hand up to her forehead dramatically and fell over sideways onto Dawn's shoulder in a fake faint.

J.J. was the lead singer for Cheddar Jam. Like the other three boys in the band, he was a senior at Wawatosa High School. At the Valentine Dance, Hannah had spent the entire time staring at him. She was crazy about the way his long hair fell into his eyes when he was singing.

"How can you be thinking about yourself at a time like this? *Hello?* I'm having a crisis here, in case you haven't noticed," Donnica complained. But Hannah seemed not to have heard her.

"If only your dad had hired Cheddar Jam," Hannah continued dreamily, "that would have been in —"

" — credible," said Dawn, finishing the word for her.

"Hey!" Donnica said, stamping her foot. "How many times do I have to tell you two? *I* do the first syllables around here. That's the rule."

"Sorry," Hannah apologized. "I was distracted." Then she put the back of her hand to her forehead again. "I can't stop thinking about J.J. — I'm telling you, if I ever get to meet him in person I one-hundred-percent guarantee —"

Donnica reached over and snatched Hannah's hand away from her forehead.

"I one-hundred-percent guarantee I'm going to strangle you if you don't stop saying that," she growled. "Don't you realize how humiliating this experience is going to be for me? There's a juggling bear coming to my birthday party."

"I have an idea," Hannah offered in an attempt to get back on Donnica's good side. "Since the party is going to be *outside*, why don't you tell Bumbles he's only allowed to juggle *inside*. That way nobody will even know he's there."

"You know, that's not a bad idea," Donnica said, brightening a little.

Hannah smiled, feeling very pleased with herself.

"Maybe you could do the same thing with Oggie," she suggested.

"Oh, don't worry about him," Donnica said. "I already came up with a plan for how to deal with Oggie Cooder. I'm just waiting for the right time to put it into action."

And that right time happened to be right around the corner.

6

*O*ggie walked home alone that afternoon. On the way he passed a repair truck from the phone company. Two men — one tall and thin, the other short and squat — were standing on the ground pointing up at the telephone wires that ran high overhead. Then the short man climbed into a large white metal box attached to a long pole on the back of the truck. A second later the box began to rise up into the air until the man was close enough to the wires to be able to reach them.

"Do you mind if I ask you what that thing is called?" Oggie asked the worker who was still standing on the ground.

"It's called a cherry picker."

Oggie laughed. "That's a funny name," he said.

"Maybe so, but it sure beats climbing a ladder, which is what we used to have to do before this thing was invented," the man replied.

"Necessity is the mother of invention," said Oggie, suddenly remembering Ms. Hepper's words.

"Did you make that up?" asked the man.

"No, some guy in Texas did," Oggie told him.

As Oggie watched the man in the cherry picker working on the wires overhead, he absentmindedly reached into his back pocket and pulled out one of the slices of processed American cheese he'd been carrying around all day. Oggie always kept a few slices of cheese in his pocket in case he felt like charving. "Charving" is a combination of the words "chewing" and "carving," and Oggie could charve cheese into the shape of just about anything he wanted. It was one of his favorite hobbies.

"What the heck are you doing with that cheese, son?" asked the worker, giving Oggie a funny look.

"Oh." Oggie held up the cheese to show the man. "I was charving your cherry picker. See?"

The man's eyes suddenly lit up with recognition. "You're that boy who was all over the newspapers a while back, aren't you? The one who was almost on that TV show." He looked at the cheese, pointed, and laughed. "Well, I'll be. That's my buddy in the bucket right there, isn't it?"

Oggie smiled and nodded. For a brief time he'd been sort of famous in Wawatosa because he'd been invited to charve on a TV show called *Hidden Talents*. In the end, though, he'd decided he wasn't cut out for Hollywood.

"Okay, George!" called the man who was up high working on the wires. "Bring 'er down."

While George worked the controls to bring his friend safely back down to the ground, Oggie asked him if he knew who had invented the cherry picker. George said he didn't, and then he asked his friend, whose name it turned out was also George.

"Nope," said the short George as he climbed out

of the bucket. "But who cares who invented it, as long as it works?"

George and George asked if they could keep the charved cherry picker Oggie had made so they could take it home to show to their kids. Oggie quickly charved a second cherry picker so they could each have one, then he left the two men admiring his cheesy handiwork and walked the rest of the way home trying to imagine what it would feel like to invent something as useful as a cherry picker.

As usual, Turk was waiting at the door when Oggie got home.

"Were you listening for my footsteps, boy?" Oggie asked as he crouched down next to Turk to give him a good belly scratch. Turk burped and rolled over onto his back, closing his eyes and wagging his tail with pleasure.

Every day after school, Oggie took Turk for a long walk. Sometimes they went to the park where Oggie would throw tennis balls for Turk to chase.

Other times they'd walk into town and drop in at Too Good to Be Threw, the resale shop that Oggie's parents owned and ran in downtown Wawatosa.

Turk knew the way to the park by heart and he knew the way to the store, too, but this time he didn't choose to go in either of those directions. Instead he pulled Oggie down the street and around the corner toward Walnut Acres, a new housing development that had sprung up in the last year or so. Oggie had never walked around there before. He thought that Walnut Acres sounded like the kind of place a squirrel might want to live.

Turk stopped to sniff at a bush in front of a house with a yellow door and a brand-new bike parked in the driveway. A boy in a red-and-white-striped shirt was leaning over, using a pump to put air in the front tire. His back was to Oggie, but when he stood up and turned around, Oggie was surprised to see who it was.

"Hi, Dylan," called Oggie. "I didn't know you lived in Walnut Acres."

"Yeah," Dylan answered. He raised his arms and smoothed his hair back with both hands, then pointed at Turk and said, "Cool dog."

Oggie walked up the driveway in order to properly introduce Turk to Dylan.

"His real name is Turkey-on-Rye," Oggie explained, "but I call him Turk for short."

Dylan bent down and scratched Turk behind the ears. In return, he got a big slobbery dog kiss on the cheek.

"Have you done your homework yet?" Oggie asked Dylan.

"Nope."

"Have you figured out what your haiku's going to be about yet?"

"Nope."

Oggie noticed something pink sticking out of Dylan's back pocket and knew right away what it was. "Are you going to Donnica's birthday party, too?" he asked.

Dylan smoothed back his hair again.

"Nope," he said. "I don't like girls."

"*Any* girls?" asked Oggie.

"Nope," Dylan replied. Then he pointed at Oggie's right foot. "Your shoe's untied."

Oggie looked down and saw that once again his right shoelace had come undone. He was going to have to measure more carefully from now on when he made his laces. Oggie looked around for a place to sit down and noticed a large red trunk sitting on the grass beside the driveway.

"Okay if I sit on this while I tie my shoe?" Oggie asked.

"Sure," said Dylan, smoothing his hair back again even though it hadn't moved a bit since the last time he'd done it.

If only Oggie had opened the lid of the red trunk instead of sitting down on it, everything might have been different. Instead he finished tying his shoelace in a triple knot, which he hoped would keep it tied once and for all. Then he stood up and walked over to Dylan, who had gone back to pumping up his bike tires.

"How about showing me your room?" Oggie said.

Dylan shrugged. "Okay."

Oggie followed Dylan into the house, leaving the red trunk and its very interesting contents behind.

7

Dylan's house was nice inside. Oggie met his mom, and she offered him a cookie.

"It doesn't have any marshmallows in it, does it?" asked Oggie.

"Are you allergic to marshmallows, Oggie?" Mrs. James seemed concerned.

"No, but I can't afford to lose any brain cells today," he explained. "I have to write a haiku later and I have a feeling it's going to be hard."

On the way up the stairs to Dylan's room, Oggie asked Dylan what he liked to do for fun.

"I'm into computers," Dylan told him. "Games and Googling stuff for fun, you know?"

Actually, Oggie didn't know. Computers were on

the list of things that his parents considered hazardous to his brain cells, so there was no Googling for fun at the Cooder house.

"Do you have any cards?" asked Oggie.

Dylan's face immediately lit up.

"You like cards?"

"You betcha," Oggie said enthusiastically. "I know a couple of good tricks I can teach you. Or we could play Old Maid. Or War."

Dylan's face fell. Oggie was obviously not thinking of the same kind of cards he was. In Chicago, Dylan's best friend had been named Bo. They'd done everything together. But since the James family had moved to Wawatosa, Dylan hadn't met anybody like Bo. Mostly he'd just been hanging around by himself, or tagging along after his older brother, Justin, when Justin wasn't too busy working.

Up in Dylan's room, Oggie learned that the cards Dylan was interested in weren't playing cards. They were called Ghouler cards, and Dylan collected them.

"I've got four hundred thirty-seven Ghorks, plus two of the four Shadow Zwills," Dylan told him proudly.

Oggie didn't have any idea what Ghorks or Shadow Zwills were, and he didn't see the point of collecting cards that you couldn't even play Old Maid with. He was, however, interested in the poster over Dylan's bed.

"Have you been to Hawaii?" he asked, admiring the picture of palm trees lining a black sandy beach.

"Yeah," said Dylan.

"I almost got a free trip to Hawaii once," Oggie told him. "I entered a contest. But I didn't win."

"Do you enter a lot of contests?" asked Dylan.

"Bazillions," said Oggie.

"Have you ever won anything?"

"Not yet. But next week I'm going to enter a birdcalling contest. I'm doing a yellow-bellied sapsucker. Want to hear?"

"Maybe later," said Dylan.

There was an awkward silence. Finally, to make conversation, Dylan said, "We went to Hawaii last Christmas. That's where I got the poster."

"My family always goes to Zanesville for Christmas," Oggie told him. "My uncle Vern can gargle 'Jingle Bells' with a mouth full of eggnog."

Dylan tried not to be too obvious about it as he snuck a quick peek at his watch. Oggie was nice, but Dylan didn't feel they had anything in common.

Downstairs a door slammed loudly.

"Yo, Little Bro!" called a deep voice.

"Up here!" yelled Dylan.

Oggie heard footsteps running up the stairs, and a minute later Dylan's older brother, Justin, opened the door. The two brothers looked a lot alike except that Justin was taller and his hair was much longer than Dylan's.

"I've gotta take my suit downtown to the cleaners. Can I borrow your bike?" Justin asked.

"Sure," Dylan said.

Justin looked at Oggie and whistled.

"Where'd you get those checkered pants, man? They're sweet."

"They're from my parents' store," Oggie told him.

"I didn't think this town had any stores that sold decent stuff like that," said Justin.

Oggie was proud of what his parents did for a living. "It's called Too Good to Be Threw," he said. "I get all my clothes from there. Except for my shoelaces. I make those myself."

Turk began to bark. Oggie had left him tied up outside because the James family had a cat. Turk felt the same way about cats as he did about paper, loose change, and dirty socks — *yum*.

"Okay, Turkey Boy, I get the message!" Oggie called out the window. Then he turned to Dylan and said, "I guess I should get going."

"Yeah," said Dylan, who still wished he could find somebody at Truman who at least knew what Ghouler cards were.

"I'd love to check out your parents' store," said

Justin, still admiring Oggie's pants. "I could really use a pair of those. But I'm so swamped I don't have any time to go shopping. I've got three jobs this weekend, plus I'm busing tables at the Clam Digger every night this week. I need all the work I can get. I'm saving up for a car."

"Tell Oggie what happened at the Clam Digger last night," Dylan said.

"Oh, some guy choked on a clam shell and I had to do the Heimlich maneuver on him."

"What's the Heimlich maneuver?" asked Oggie.

Justin put his arms around Dylan's middle to demonstrate.

"You put your fists together in the front like this, squeeze hard, and then watch out, because whatever the person's choking on comes flying out like a rocket."

"Neat-o!" said Oggie.

"Not as neat-o as those checkered pants you've got on, little dude," said Justin.

"If you want, I can ask my mom if she has any more like these at the store. If she does, I could bring them to you," Oggie offered. "What size do you wear?"

Justin told Oggie what size he wore and thanked him.

"I owe you one, man," he said.

Little did he know how soon he would be repaying the favor.

8

On his way out, Oggie stopped to say good-bye to Mrs. James and to thank her for the cookie.

"I hope you'll come visit Dylan again," she said with a smile. "He could use a nice friend like you. We bought him that bike hoping he'd ride around the neighborhood and explore a little, but all he seems to want to do is stay up in his room on the computer."

On the way home Oggie decided to practice his yellow-bellied sapsucker call. His interest in bird-calling had begun when his aunt Hettie sent him something called a Swiss Warbler. It was a small leather half-moon-shaped device that you put on your tongue. There was a tiny piece of cellophane on one side of it, and if you hissed air across it in just the right way, you could make very realistic-sounding chirps and twitters.

The yellow-bellied sapsucker has three different calls: *KWEE-URK kwee-urk*, which means "stay away from me," *week-week wurp-wurp*, which means "I like you," and *k-waan k-waan*, which means "I'm very excited."

As he turned the corner and started up Tullahoma Street, Oggie was concentrating hard on his *kwee-urk*. Mrs. Perfecto, who was standing out on her front lawn, staring at the bushes growing in front of her house, heard the strange sound and, seeing that it was Oggie, waved him over.

"Is your mother at home?" she asked anxiously.

"*Shleeze shill esh ush shorsh,*" said Oggie, forgetting that he still had the Swiss Warbler in his mouth. Realizing his mistake, he quickly pulled it out and repeated his response. "She's still at the store."

"Oh," said Mrs. Perfecto, nervously eyeing the spitty Swiss Warbler in Oggie's hand. "Perhaps I'll give her a call later and see if she can stop by."

Turk started tugging on his leash. He was clearly interested in sniffing the Perfectos' bushes, but Oggie thought that might not be a great idea, especially with Mrs. Perfecto standing right there. He popped the Swiss Warbler back in his mouth so that he'd have both hands free to keep Turk on the sidewalk.

Mrs. Perfecto looked over at her bushes again and sighed. She was very worried. The Garden Club committee could stop by without warning at any time to inspect her yard. It just wouldn't do to have raggedy rhododendrons. She needed Isabel Cooder's help, and there wasn't a minute to spare.

Turning back to Oggie, Mrs. Perfecto smiled. "By the way," she said, a little more sweetly than was necessary, "did you receive the invitation to Donnica's party? I do hope your mother is aware that you've been invited, dear."

At the mention of Donnica's birthday party,

Oggie attempted to *prrrrr-ip!* But because of the Swiss Warbler in his mouth, it came out sounding more like a squawk.

Mrs. Perfecto was so startled by the sound that she put her hand to her heart.

"Oh, my!" she exclaimed.

Oggie pulled the spitty warbler out of his mouth once more.

"I wouldn't miss the party for anything," he told Mrs. Perfecto happily. "But I do have a question I need to ask Donnica. Is she home by any chance?"

"Why, yes. She's upstairs with her friends. Just a second and I'll get her for you." Mrs. Perfecto lifted her head and yelled at the top of her lungs, "DONNICA!"

A few seconds later an upstairs window slid open and Donnica stuck her head out.

Oggie waved up at her.

"Ewww," said Donnica, wrinkling her nose in disgust. "What are you doing here?"

"Mind your manners," scolded Mrs. Perfecto quickly. She couldn't afford to have her daughter being rude to Isabel Cooder's son — not with her rhododendrons looking the way they did. "Be polite, Cupcake. Our wonderful little neighbor here has something he needs to ask you."

"I was just wondering if you figured out yet what you want me to get you for your birthday," Oggie called up.

"Isn't that lovely?" cried Mrs. Perfecto.

Donnica's blue eyes narrowed slightly, like a cat preparing to pounce on a mouse. This was the moment she'd been waiting for.

"Come on up," she called down to Oggie in the same overly sweet voice her mother had just been using.

Knowing she only had a short time before Oggie got to her room, Donnica quickly pulled her head inside and closed the window. Then she turned to Dawn and Hannah, who were sitting next to each other on the big pink canopy bed.

"Remember that little plan I told you about?" she asked them. "Well, get ready because the time has come to put it into action."

"What do you want us to do?" asked Hannah.

"Nothing. Just leave the talking to me."

Oggie had never been inside the Perfectos' house before, but Mrs. Perfecto told him to go up the stairs and that Donnica's room would be the third door on the left.

"Can I bring my dog in with me?" he asked.

Mrs. Perfecto shuddered at the thought of a giant, hairy dog walking around on her nice clean carpets, but then she glanced at her raggedy rhododendrons and reconsidered.

"The Cooders are *all* welcome in our home," Mrs. Perfecto told him, quickly adding, "Make sure to tell your mother that I said that, won't you, dear?"

When Oggie reached the top of the stairs, he turned left and began to count. The first door he passed was the bathroom. Next to it was a narrow door that looked like some kind of a closet. The third door was closed and had a pink heart with a letter *D* painted on it.

Oggie knocked and Donnica told him to come in. As he opened the door and stepped inside, he tripped over the end of that pesky right shoelace, which had come undone again despite the triple knot. Oggie did his best to regain his balance, flapping his arms like a giant albatross, but despite his efforts, he ended up sprawled on Donnica's fuzzy pink rug with his head resting on the toe of her right shoe.

Donnica quickly pulled her foot out from under Oggie's head, letting it smoosh into the carpet. Oggie sat up and began to retie his shoelace — this time in a quadruple knot — while Turk made himself at home, sniffing around the room for a minute before settling down next to Oggie on the rug.

Donnica flashed Hannah and Dawn a watch-this kind of a look.

"Oggie" she began, "I think we need to have a little talk."

"Okay," Oggie said, smiling up at her.

"See, there's something you should know about my birthday party."

"*Prrrrr-ip! Prrrrr-ip!*" went Oggie. He couldn't help it. Every time the subject of the party came up, he felt happy all over again.

"Is there something you want to tell me about your present?" Oggie asked. "'Cause I want to get you something you really, really —"

"No!" Donnica put up a hand to stop him. "This is not about my present." She paused to sit down on the bed between Hannah and Dawn, who quickly scooted over to make room for her. "I want to talk to you about the B.P.R.'s."

"B.P.R.'s?" said Oggie.

"Birthday Party Rules," Donnica explained.

"You never had rules at any of your birthday parties before," blurted Dawn, forgetting the instruction she'd been given to keep quiet.

Donnica immediately jammed her elbow into Dawn's ribs hard enough to make her jump.

"Of course I did. You remember the rules, *don't you, Dawn*?" Donnica said pointedly.

"I do now," Dawn muttered, rubbing her tender ribs.

"Anyway," Donnica continued, turning her attention back to Oggie, "I thought I'd better tell you about the rules ahead of time since this is the first time you've ever come to one of my parties."

"All right," Oggie agreed.

But the truth was, as Dawn had said, there had never been any birthday party rules before. Donnica's big plan was to invent a bunch of rules she knew it would be impossible for Oggie to follow.

"If you can't follow the rules, you can't come to my party," she informed Oggie.

"Okay," he said. He'd never heard of birthday party rules before, but was certainly willing to do whatever it took in order to be allowed to come to Donnica's party and swim in her pool.

"Are you ready for Rule Number One?" Donnica asked Oggie.

"Ready," he told her.

Donnica held up a pink-glitter-polish-tipped finger. "NO *prrrrr-ip-ing* ALLOWED."

9

Donnica was delighted to see the worried look on Oggie's face. Her plan was working already!

"No *prrrrr-ip-ing*?" Oggie asked. "Gee, that might be kind of hard. See, I don't do it on purpose, it just pops out accidentally when I'm feeling happy."

"Well, it's not allowed to pop out at my party," said Donnica, folding her arms across her chest. "So if you can't control it, you can't come."

Oggie couldn't bear the thought of missing Donnica's party. There had to be something he could do to keep from *prrrrr-ip-ing* while he was there. When he got the hiccups he always held his breath or put sugar under his tongue. Maybe that would work. Or maybe if he *prrrrr-ip-ed* a whole bunch right before the party, he'd be all *prrr-rr-ip-ed* out when he got there.

"I'll figure something out," Oggie told Donnica. "Is that the only rule?"

Donnica shook her head and put up a second finger.

"Rule Number Two: NO CROCHETED SHOE-LACES ALLOWED."

Oggie looked down at his feet. The quadruple knot he'd tied was still holding tight.

"I don't have any regular shoelaces," he said. "But I guess I could buy some, or maybe I could just wear slippers. I've got a pair of really nice fuzzy ones. They've got pom-poms on the toes. Are pom-poms allowed?"

Oggie's parents' store specialized in used clothing of all kinds. "Vintage," his mother called it. Donnica knew that almost everything in Oggie's wardrobe came from the store, which is why she was ready with Rule Number Three.

"NO USED CLOTHES ALLOWED," she

said. "And in case you're wondering, that includes bathing suits."

Instead of being upset by this, Oggie broke into a huge grin.

"No prob-lemio with the bathing suit-io!" he cried happily. "My mom just bought me a pair of swim trunks on sale at Selznick's department store. They're red with pineapples on them and they've even got pockets. And if I can't figure out what to wear on my feet I can always just come barefoot."

The plan was not working quite as well as Donnica had hoped, but she was not ready to give up yet. She was determined to keep Oggie Cooder away from her birthday party, no matter how many rules she had to come up with.

"Sorry," she said, holding up a fourth glitter-tipped finger. "Rule Number Four: NO RED BATHING SUITS ALLOWED."

"Really?" said Hannah, who had gotten so caught up in Donnica's rules, she'd forgotten they weren't real. She was worried about the fact that the bathing suit she was planning to wear to the party was also red. One sharp look from Donnica brought her quickly back to her senses just in time to save herself from a painful jab in the ribs.

"How many rules are there?" asked Oggie.

As many as it takes, thought Donnica, and she began to tick things off on her fingers.

"No tripping over your feet, no cheese charving, no talking about boring inventions, no Uncle Vern stories, no dorky, made-up words like 'yeppers' or 'bazillion,' no warnings about things that can ruin your brain cells, no dogs allowed — especially big hairy ones that are named after sandwiches. No bird imitations —"

When she said that, Oggie's eyes got very wide.

"Uh-oh," he said, suddenly looking very worried. "I think we have a problem."

Donnica smiled. It had taken a little longer than anticipated, but her plan was finally working. Oggie Cooder had realized that he would never be able to follow all the rules she had come up with. Ah, sweet victory!

But then something strange happened. Oggie got down on his hands and knees and began crawling around on the floor, frantically lifting up the edges of the rug and peering under the furniture.

"What in the world are you doing?" asked Donnica.

"I'm looking for my Swiss Warbler," Oggie explained. "I must have dropped it when I tripped. I have to find it. I can't do my yellow-bellied sap-sucker without it!"

Tweeeeeeet!

Oggie sat up and looked at Donnica.

"What are you looking at me for?" she said. "I didn't make that sound."

He looked at Dawn and Hannah, but they both shook their heads.

Tweeeeeeeeeeeeeeeeet!

"Oh, no!" cried Oggie when he saw who was making the sound. "What did you do, Turkey Boy?"

Turk, who was sitting by the door, wagged his tail and tried to look innocent, but the

whistling sound coming from his mouth gave him away.

He'd found the Swiss Warbler on the floor and had swallowed it. Now it was stuck in his throat!

Oggie quickly stood up. This was not the first time Turk had eaten something he wasn't supposed to. In fact, it had happened often enough that Oggie already knew the drill.

"I have to go home right away and call the vet, in case I need to bring Turk in to see him," he said.

Donnica was not happy. She was convinced her plan had been about to work, and she wanted to finish what she had begun.

"We have to go over the rest of the rules," she said.

"I don't have time right now," Oggie told her. "I have to call the vet. Besides, I have a terrible memory. Why don't you write down all the rules and bring the list to school with you tomorrow, okay?"

Turk let out another loud *tweeeet!* followed by

about a dozen high-pitched *chirps*, and Oggie hurried off with him.

"Are you sure this plan of yours is going to work?" Dawn asked after Oggie had left. "He seemed a lot more worried about his dog than he did about your party rules."

"Shows what you know," Donnica said with a superior smile.

To be honest, though, a minute earlier Donnica had been feeling worried about the plan, too. But she wasn't as worried anymore. She'd just been handed the secret weapon she'd been searching for — an Oggie-proof rule.

10

The minute Oggie got home, he called the vet and explained what had happened.

"It's probably nothing to worry about," Dr. Roberts told him. "Just feed him a few slices of bread. That ought to knock it loose."

Turk was more than happy to cooperate, but even after he wolfed down four slices of bread, the Swiss Warbler was still stuck in his throat. He didn't seem to be in any pain, and when Oggie checked back with the vet, Dr. Roberts said to give it a little more time and a lot more bread. Oggie decided there was no point in worrying. He decided the same thing about the B.P.R.'s. As long as Donnica brought the list to school in the morning, he'd have enough time to go over it before the party. On

Saturday he would simply bring the list with him in case he needed to refresh his memory about any of the rules.

For years Oggie had sat on his porch steps listening to the laughter and splashing and happy shrieks coming over the high wooden fence that surrounded the Perfectos' swimming pool. He wasn't about to let a few silly rules keep him from finding out how it felt to be on the other side of the fence for a change.

At dinner that night, Oggie told his parents that Donnica had invited him to her birthday party.

"How nice!" said Mrs. Cooder. "The Perfectos have been a lot more friendly lately, have you noticed? Why, just the other day Miriam Perfecto, who never even used to wave when she saw me, practically kissed me when I suggested that all she needed to perk up her begonias was a few handfuls of eggshells."

"Why don't slugs like eggshells?" asked Oggie.

"I suppose they don't like having their tender little bellies scratched," Mrs. Cooder explained.

"I guess that makes you the opposite of a slug, huh, Turkey Boy?" said Oggie, reaching down and giving his dog a quick belly scratch.

Turk rolled over on his back and let out a satisfied *tweeeeeeeeet!*

After helping to clear the dinner table, Oggie went to his room and settled in to finish his homework. He'd already done the math problems and had looked over the spelling words. The only thing he had left to do was to write his haiku. Usually when Oggie had to come up with an idea for a story to write during Creative Writing, he thought about interesting things that had happened to him — like the time he got his toe caught in the bathtub faucet, and his mother had to use a whole stick of butter to make it slippery enough to pull it out. Or the time Turk sat down on a bottle of glue and ended up with his rear end stuck to the carpet.

But Turk's rear end didn't seem like the right kind of thing to write a haiku about, especially since the poem was supposed to be about Oggie. He thought about trying to use the word *prrrrr-ip* in his haiku, but he couldn't decide whether to count it as one syllable or two, so he figured it would be safer not to use it at all. Oggie tried and tried to figure out how to describe the most important thing about himself, his *essence*, but the more he thought about it, the harder it seemed to get.

"What are you working on, son?" asked Mr. Cooder, sticking his head in the doorway to see how Oggie was doing.

"Haiku," said Oggie.

"Gesundheit!" said Mr. Cooder.

Oggie laughed at the joke. Haiku *did* sound a lot like *achoo*.

"It's a kind of a poem," Oggie explained. "And I have to write one."

"Sorry, Ogg. I'm not a very poetic guy," said Mr. Cooder. "That's more your mother's department. Want me to send out an S.O.S.?"

"What's an S.O.S.?" Oggie asked.

"That's a signal you send out when you're in trouble. In Morse code it's *dot dot dot dash dash dash dot dot dot*."

Oggie had heard of Morse code. Samuel Morse, the man it was named after, was one of the inventors in the book Oggie had taken out of the library.

"Okay," Oggie told his dad. "Go ahead and send out an S.O.S. I can use all the help I can get."

Mrs. Cooder came in a few minutes later.

"Your father tells me you need a little help with a haiku," she said. "I remember writing those in grade school. What is the pattern again?"

"Five, seven, five," Oggie told her.

"What are you going to write about?" Oggie's mother asked. "Cherry blossoms and mist-covered mountains?"

"No. I'm supposed to write about my essence," Oggie explained, quickly adding, "but not the kind of essence Uncle Vern has in his armpits."

"Thank goodness." Mrs. Cooder laughed. "What have you written so far?"

"Nothing," Oggie confessed. "I'm kind of stuck."

"Sometimes when I'm looking for inspiration, I stand on my head," Mrs. Cooder told him.

"Does it work?" Oggie asked. He had seen his mother stand on her head many times, but had never thought to ask her why.

"It certainly gets the blood circulating," she said. "Why don't you try it and see what happens? Just be careful not to fall over."

After Oggie's mother left, he pulled the pillow off his bed and put it on the floor. But the minute he tried standing on his head, Turk came running over and knocked him down. Turk thought this was a great game, but Oggie had work to do, so after it happened again, Oggie kicked Turk out of the room and closed the door. Then he placed the top of his head in the middle of the pillow and pushed himself up into a headstand.

Turk whined and scratched at the door while Oggie stood on his head and tried to think about his essence. "Who am I?" he asked himself again

and again. His face turned bright red as the blood rushed to his head, but it didn't seem to be helping with the haiku. Then, just as he was about to give up, an idea appeared from out of nowhere, like magic.

"That's it!" Oggie cried as he toppled over onto the carpet.

Ten minutes later Oggie's haiku was not only finished, it was neatly folded and tucked into his backpack ready to bring to school.

11

The next morning, Oggie ran into Donnica, Dawn, and Hannah on their way to school. They were talking about the haiku they'd written for the assignment.

"Mine is totally me," said Donnica proudly. "In other words, *per* —"

Dawn and Hannah hesitated.

"*Per* —" Donnica prompted again.

"— sonal?" Hannah said uncertainly.

"No," said Donnica disgustedly. "Not *personal*. *Perfect*. My haiku is perfect. Perfection is totally my essence."

"I couldn't think of anything at first," Oggie told the girls. "But then I stood on my head. It was kind of like the Heimlich maneuver — you know, that squeezing thing you're supposed to do when some-one's choking? — except instead of a clam shell, a haiku came flying out."

The girls looked at one another.

"Loo —" mouthed Donnica silently to Hannah and Dawn.

"— zer" Hannah and Dawn mouthed back.

"So did you bring the list?" Oggie asked Donnica.

Donnica reached into her backpack and pulled out several sheets of paper, neatly stapled together. "B.P.R." was written in large pink letters across the top of the first page. Before she handed the list to Oggie, Donnica took out a pen and added one more rule.

"'Rule Number One Hundred and One,'" she said as she wrote, "'NO STANDING ON YOUR HEAD ALLOWED.'"

When she finished, she gave the list to Oggie.

"If I were you, I'd stay away from those orange apricots," she told him. "You're going to need all the brain cells you've got if you're going to have these rules memorized by Saturday."

Oggie stopped dead in his tracks.

"*Memorized?*" he said. "You didn't say anything about memorizing."

"Didn't I?" There was a gleam in Donnica's eyes. "Well, it's right here. See?" Donnica pointed to the last page of her list. "'Rule Number One Hundred, *All* Birthday Party Rules must be memorized.' And you'll have to be able to prove it, too."

"Prove it?" Oggie gulped.

"Yes — I give all my party guests a little quiz before they're even allowed to come in the door. Right, girls?"

Dawn and Hannah nodded like a couple of bobbleheads on a dashboard.

Oggie was pretty sure he could manage to keep from *prrrrr-ip-ing* if he put his mind to it. He could go to the party barefoot instead of wearing shoes or slippers. And it wouldn't be hard to exchange his red bathing suit for another color. But memorizing was another matter. Oggie had trouble memorizing the weekly spelling words, and there were only ten of those. There was absolutely no way he was going to be able to memorize a hundred and one rules by Saturday. Oggie was not going to be able to go to Donnica's birthday party.

And as that disappointing thought entered Oggie's head, something occurred in Wawatosa, Wisconsin, that had never happened before: Donnica Perfecto and Oggie Cooder were thinking the exact same thing.

Kids were already beginning to go inside when Oggie reached the schoolyard. Amy Schneider waved to him from the top of the steps, but he didn't see her. As Oggie walked down the hall toward his classroom, all he could think about was the fun he was going to be missing. What if there were piggies-in-a-blanket? Oggie's aunt Hettie always served those when she had a party. They were delicious little hot dogs rolled up in dough with toothpicks stuck through them. Oggie's uncle

Vern loved them, too, and had once eaten six-ty-seven of them in one sitting — including the toothpicks.

Oggie's mouth watered thinking about those piggies-in-a-blanket, but it looked like his imagina-tion was as close as he was going to get to mini–hot dogs now that Donnica had informed him that the rules for her party had to be memorized.

Oggie felt so miserable, Mr. Snolinovsky didn't have to speak to him once about *prrrrr-ip-ing* during class. What was there to *prrrrr-ip* about? A dark cloud hung over Oggie's head all morning, until suddenly, right before lunch, he had a brain-storm. Oggie and Amy sometimes quizzed each other on spelling words. Working together made it much easier. Since Amy was going to Donnica's party, too, maybe they could team up and work together on memorizing the rules!

"I was thinking maybe we should get ready for Donnica's party together," Oggie said the minute Amy sat down at the lunch table.

But Amy got the exact same uncomfortable look

on her face that she'd had the day before when the topic of Donnica's party had come up.

"What's the matter?" Oggie asked.

"Did Donnica really invite you to her party?"

"Yeppers," said Oggie. "I'd show you the invitation, but Turk ate it. He ate my Swiss Warbler, too. I'll tell you about that later. First I want to know if you want to help each other get ready."

"Um. I don't think so," Amy said.

"Why not?"

"Well, for one thing, I'm not going to the party."

"Why not? Don't you like girls either?"

Amy gave him a funny look.

"That's why Dylan isn't going," Oggie explained. "He doesn't like girls. He only likes Ghorks."

Amy gave Oggie an even funnier look.

"Ghorks?"

"Yeah," said Oggie, "Ghorks and windowsills. Or something like that. Anyway, how come you're not coming to the party?"

"Because I didn't get invited," said Amy.

"You didn't?" Oggie was genuinely surprised. He had assumed that since Donnica had invited him, she must have invited everybody in the class. "Maybe your invitation got lost in the mail," Oggie said to Amy. "Do you want me to ask Donnica to send you a new one?"

"No," Amy said quickly. "I don't really want to go to Donnica's birthday party. We're not exactly friends, you know."

Oggie felt that dark cloud sliding back into place over his head. If Amy wasn't coming to the party, that meant he was back at square one. He knew he would never be able to memorize all of the rules by himself.

Now it was Amy's turn to ask Oggie what was wrong.

"I was finally going to get a chance to dive into Donnica's pool," Oggie explained sadly, "but now that I can't go to the party, it's probably never going to happen."

"Why can't you go to the party?" Amy asked. "You were invited, weren't you? And you sure seemed excited about it yesterday when you found out about Bumbles."

"I know. But there's no way I'm going to be able to get ready by myself."

"I don't get it," said Amy. "Why do you need help getting ready for a pool party? All you have to do is put on your bathing suit and walk across the street."

"Actually, I can't wear my bathing suit," said Oggie. "It's red. Rule Number Four is no red bathing suits allowed."

"*What?*" said Amy.

"There's a whole list of rules. A hundred and one of them. And I just found out that I have to have them all memorized by Saturday or Donnica says I can't come to the party."

Amy was beginning to get the picture. She hadn't wanted to say anything, but she'd actually been pretty surprised to hear that Oggie had been invited to Donnica's party. It was clear from the way Donnica acted that she didn't like Oggie. So why invite him to the party? Amy was sure there was something fishy going on.

"Where is this list of rules?" she asked.

Oggie pulled Donnica's B.P.R.'s out of his back pocket and handed it across the table to Amy. As Amy began to read, her cheeks turned very pink. She saw right through Donnica's little plan. Obviously Donnica didn't really want Oggie at her party. Tricking him into thinking he had to follow all these rules was just plain mean.

"I can't believe this," Amy said.

"I know," said Oggie. "There's no way I'll ever be able to memorize them all by Saturday."

"Oh, I wouldn't be so sure about that," said Amy.

And suddenly Donnica Perfecto wasn't the only one with a plan.

12

After lunch, Oggie felt a lot better. Amy had promised she would figure out a way to help him get ready for the party. Mr. Snolinovsky collected the homework from the day before. But instead of putting the haiku in his red folder, where he put the rest of the work to be checked, he asked everybody to fold the poems in half and come up one at a time to place each one in a special box he had brought in and placed on the corner of his desk. The box was covered with colorful paper — a background of blue sky decorated with rainbows.

Oggie carefully folded his poem in half, and when it was his turn, he went up and slipped it into the box. Amy came after him, but before she returned to her seat she stopped to admire the pictures on the box.

"I love rainbows," she said.

"Richard of York Gave Battle in Vain," Mr. Snolinovsky replied.

"Pardon?" said Amy politely.

"It's a trick to help you remember the order of the colors in the rainbow," said Mr. Snolinovsky. "I learned it back when I was in grade school and never forgot it. Richard of York Gave Battle in Vain: red, orange, yellow, green, blue, indigo, violet."

"Cool!" said Amy enthusiastically — not because she had learned a new way to remember the colors in the rainbow, but because it had just given her a great idea for how to help Oggie.

During Silent Reading that afternoon, Oggie searched through the book he'd taken out of the library the day before, in hopes of finding the name of the person who had invented the cherry picker. He didn't find what he was looking for, but during his search he did discover that an

American dentist named Edward Angle was the person most people considered responsible for having invented braces. He would have to remember to tell Amy.

As Oggie closed his book and was about to put it away in his desk, Amy happened to walk by. She was on her way to sharpen her pencil in the electric sharpener Mr. Snolinovsky kept on the windowsill, but as she passed Oggie's desk she slowed down and slipped him a note. Oggie unfolded the little triangle of paper and read:

CAN YOU COME OVER THIS AFTERNOON
AFTER SCHOOL?

The only plans Oggie had for after school were to do his homework and take Turk for a walk.

"So, can you come?" Amy asked Oggie later as they were walking down the hall together after the last bell.

"Sure, I can. But I have to walk Turk first," Oggie said.

"You can bring him with you, if you want. I'll put Jitters in the laundry room. That way Turk won't try to eat her like last time."

Jitters was Amy's cat, and she made Turk's mouth water the same way Oggie's did when he thought about piggies-in-a-blanket.

"Speaking of eating, should I have a snack before I come over to your house?" Oggie asked. He crossed his fingers and hoped like crazy that Amy would say no. Unlike Oggie's mother, who insisted that Oggie have a healthy snack after school every day — something like raisins or carrot sticks — Amy's mother was not as strict. Oggie was particularly fond of her root beer floats.

"My mom said something about making brownies this afternoon," Amy told Oggie. "And there's always plenty of vanilla ice cream in the freezer if we want to have root beer floats."

Prrrrr-ip! Prrrrr-ip! Oggie (and his sweet tooth) were very happy to hear this news.

"I'll see you in about a half hour, then," said Oggie.

"Okay," said Amy. "Oh, and make sure you bring that list of rules with you when you come."

"Are you sure you don't mind helping me even though you're not invited to the party?" asked Oggie.

"You don't understand," said Amy. "Nothing in the world would give me more pleasure than knowing that you're going to be showing up on Donnica's doorstep on Saturday with all of her silly rules memorized. I'm just sorry I won't be there to see the look on her face."

"I could take a picture," Oggie offered.

Oggie and Amy parted ways and Oggie walked the rest of the way home by himself. He looked for the two Georges, but they must have been working on telephone wires in another neighborhood that day. He would have liked to watch them use the cherry picker again.

Mrs. Cooder was in the kitchen, washing lettuce at the sink when Oggie walked in the door.

"Would you like a snack, Ogg?" she called to him. "I could make you some ants on a log."

Ants on a log = celery sticks with peanut butter and raisins on top. Very healthy.

"No, thanks!" Oggie called back. "I'm going to walk Turk over to Amy's house in a minute. Her mom's making brownies."

"Come here a second first, will you?" said Oggie's mother. "I want to talk to you about something."

Oggie sincerely hoped she wasn't going to try to talk him into eating ants on a log instead of brownies.

Turk, who had been waiting eagerly at the door for Oggie as usual, was prancing around with his leash in his mouth. The Swiss Warbler was still stuck in his throat, but it must have shifted a little because in addition to tweeting and chirping, he could now twitter.

"Just a minute, Turkey Boy," Oggie told him.

Mrs. Cooder put the last of the lettuce in the salad spinner and turned off the water.

"How was school today?" she asked.

"Fine," said Oggie. "I didn't spill my chocolate milk at lunch."

"Did Mr. Snolinovsky like your haiku?"

"Oh, he didn't read it yet. We had to put them all in this box and we're going to do something special with them tomorrow."

"That's nice." Mrs. Cooder walked over to the fridge and dried her hands on the striped dish towel that was hanging from the door handle. "You know, Donnica's birthday party is the day after tomorrow. Some cute little vintage purses came into the store today. Maybe she'd like something like that."

"I don't think I should pick out a present for her until I know for sure whether I'm going to be able to go to the party," said Oggie.

"Why wouldn't you be able to go to the party?" asked Mrs. Cooder.

Oggie pulled the list of rules out of his back pocket and held it out to his mother. But before she could reach for it, Turk jumped up and snatched the

papers away, running out of the room with the list clamped tightly between his sharp teeth.

"Turk! Come back here!" cried Oggie, running after him.

The phone rang and Mrs. Cooder went to answer it while Oggie chased Turk around the couch, diving over the cushions in an attempt to retrieve the papers.

"Excuse me?" said Oggie's mother into the phone. "You'll have to repeat that. I'm afraid we have a bad connection. Who did you say was calling?"

While his mother talked on the phone, Oggie continued to chase Turk, finally managing to corner him and remove the list from his mouth. It was still in one piece, though a bit soggy in places. Turk wriggled free and ran off to find his leash, returning a minute later to drop it at Oggie's feet.

When Oggie made no move to leave, Turk, who was not used to having to wait so long for his afternoon walk, threw back his head and began to howl in frustration. Because of the Swiss Warbler in his throat, the howls came out sounding like *Kweeeeeeeee-urk! Kweeeeeeeee-urk!*

"Hey," cried Oggie, "you sound just like a yellow-bellied sapsucker!"

Turk *Kweeeeeeeee-urk-ed* again, but then Mrs. Cooder put her hand over the phone and called from the kitchen, "Take him outside, will you please, Ogg? I can't hear a thing over all that racket."

So Oggie stuck the list of B.P.R.'s back in his pocket, and he and Turk headed off to Amy's house . . . where Oggie hoped a plate of warm brownies would be waiting.

13

Turk was so happy to finally be outside that he took off on a tear, pulling Oggie along behind him like a caboose on a runaway train. As they flew past the entrance to Walnut Acres, Oggie suddenly remembered that he had promised to ask his mom if there were any checked pants left at the store in Dylan's brother's size. Oggie shook his head. Why was it so hard for him to remember things? He sure hoped that Amy was going to be able to help him memorize the B.P.R.'s.

Amy was waiting for Oggie on the front steps when he got there.

"Come here, Turkey Burger," she called, patting her knees with her hands. Turk ran up the steps and began licking her face with his big wet tongue. Amy wrinkled her nose. "Somebody around here could really use a breath mint."

"Who, me?" asked Oggie, cupping a hand over his mouth and sniffing.

Amy giggled.

"I was talking about Turk. Come on in. Jitters is already in the laundry room, so the coast is clear."

Amy's house smelled delicious.

"Hello, Oggie." Mrs. Schneider poked her head around the corner and waved. "Would you like a warm brownie?"

"Does my uncle Vern have eleven toes?" Oggie cried happily.

Mrs. Schneider looked alarmed.

"That's just Oggie's way of saying yes," Amy explained. She knew all about Oggie *and* his uncle Vern's extra toe.

"So did you bring the list?" Amy asked once they'd settled in on the couch in the den with a plate of brownies between them and two big root beer floats with red bendy straws sticking out of the creamy foam.

Oggie pulled the list out of his pocket and, careful to keep it out of Turk's reach this time, handed it to Amy.

"I think I should warn you," Oggie said, "my memory has been worse than ever lately. Do you think it could have anything to do with all those marshmallows I ate the last time we were in Ohio? Uncle Vern was trying to break his record for how many marshmallows he could throw into another person's mouth without missing."

"How many did you eat?" asked Amy.

"Fifty-three. Fifty-four if you count the cotton ball he threw in there by accident."

Amy laughed and took a sip of her root beer float.

"Shall we get started?" she asked.

Oggie groaned and slapped his forehead.

"What's the matter?" Amy asked.

"I just remembered I forgot to bring index cards

so we could make flash cards for the rules like we always do with the spelling words."

"I've got index cards," said Amy.

"One hundred and one of them?" asked Oggie doubtfully.

"We won't need nearly that many," said Amy.

"How come? I have to memorize all the rules, you know."

Amy smiled.

"Richard of York Gave Battle in Vain," she said.

"Who's Richard of York?" asked Oggie, confused. "Is he coming to Donnica's party?"

"No. 'Richard of York Gave Battle in Vain' is a trick for how to remember the order of the colors in the rainbow: red, orange, yellow, green, blue, indigo, violet."

"Neat-o," said Oggie.

"Yeah," said Amy. "And colors aren't the only thing it works for either." She studied the B.P.R.'s for a minute and then put down the list. "Putting Salad Under the Couch Is Very Messy and Dangerous," she told Oggie.

"Is there really a rule that says you're not allowed to put salad under the couch?" asked Oggie.

"No." Amy laughed. "Each word in the sentence stands for one of the rules. See?" She got a sheet of paper and wrote the letters *P, S, U, T, C, I, V, M, A,* and *D* down the side. Then next to each letter she wrote one of the rules from Donnica's list.

P —NO **PRRRRR-IP-ING**

S — NO CROCHETED **SHOELACES**

U —NO **USED** CLOTHES

T —NO **TRIPPING** OVER YOUR OWN FEET

C —NO **CHARVING**

I —NO TALKING ABOUT **INVENTORS**

V —NO UNCLE **VERN** STORIES

M —NO **MADE-UP** WORDS

A —NO **ANIMAL** IMITATIONS

D —NO **DOGS**

"Oh, I get it!" said Oggie. "This one sentence will help me remember" — he stopped and counted — "ten rules!"

"Now close your eyes and tell me what the sentence was," Amy prompted.

Oggie closed his eyes and rattled it off without a bit of trouble.

"*Putting salad under the couch is very messy and dangerous.* Hey! I remembered!"

Soon enough, he and Amy were pleased to discover that with a little practice, Oggie was also able to remember all ten of the rules the sentence represented.

"I knew it would work!" Amy cried happily. "Now all we have to do is make up funny sentences to help you remember the rest of the rules."

Which is exactly what they did.

That night Oggie went to sleep with a smile on his face. He and Amy had had a great time making up funny sentences to help him remember Donnica's rules. His two favorites were "Some People Enjoy Hot Mustard Ice Cream For Lunch On Wednesdays" and "Fish Don't Fly In Airplanes Unless They Lose Their Bicycles." Of course,

Oggie would still need to spend time going over what all of the letters in the sentences stood for, but things had gone so well with Amy, he was sure that by Saturday he would be ready. He was going to Donnica's party!

On Friday morning, Oggie woke up in a great mood. He walked Turk, grabbed a couple of slices of cheese out of the fridge, and headed off to school. He looked for Amy as soon as he got to the schoolyard, eventually spotting her sitting on a swing, reading a book.

"Can you quiz me?" he asked. "I keep forgetting the NO ANIMAL IMITATIONS rule. I think it's because I don't really do animal imitations, I do birdcalls. At least I used to, before Turk swallowed my Swiss Warbler."

Just then Donnica appeared at the edge of the yard, with Dawn and Hannah at her sides.

"I can't wait to tell Donnica I'm going to be able to come to her party after all," said Oggie. "Hey, Donnica! Guess what?"

But Amy tugged on Oggie's sleeve to hold him back.

"Don't you think it would be more fun if you surprised her?" she said.

"*Prrrrr-ip! Prrrrr-ip!* Good idea," said Oggie.

But Donnica was not the only one who was about to be surprised.

14

As soon as he walked into the classroom, Oggie noticed that the rainbow-covered box was no longer sitting on Mr. Snolinovsky's desk. He also noticed that the bulletin board at the front of the room was completely covered with colored squares of paper that hadn't been there the day before. When he went to have a closer look, Oggie discovered that each piece of paper had three lines typed on it. Haiku!

Oggie searched for his poem, finally locating it on a square of green paper, pinned to the upper right-hand corner of the board.

"There's mine!" he cried happily.

"Don't say another word, Oggie!" Mr. Snolinovsky called from his desk. "Come have a seat so I can explain what we're going to be doing with the haiku."

Once the class was seated and attendance had been taken, Mr. Snolinovsky told everybody that the reason the haiku had been typed up and put on the bulletin board was because they were going to play a game called Whose Haiku Are You?

"As you know, there are no names on the poems, and they have all been typed up so that nobody will be able to guess an author based on his or her penmanship."

"How do you play the game?" asked America.

"You'll have all day today to read the poems and think about who wrote them," Mr. Snolinovsky explained. "This afternoon you'll make your guesses."

"What do we get if we win?" asked David Korben.

"Your reward will be the joy of knowing that you are a thoughtful reader, and that you know your classmates well," Mr. Snolinovsky told him.

"Some prize," grumbled David, who was used to being handed a shiny trophy for his efforts on the basketball court.

Throughout the day, Oggie went and stood in front of the bulletin board, studying the haiku. Some of them were easy to figure out:

Basketball is cool
Cooler than baseball or foot-
Ball or golf. The end.

Although Oggie didn't think it sounded very haiku-ish the way the lines were all choppy and split up, he had to admit it did capture the essence of David Korben, who was clearly the author. Donnica's, as promised, was all about how perfect she was:

How lucky to be
So beautiful and perfect
Don't you envy me?

Bethie Hudson's was about winning a spelling bee — something she never missed an opportunity to remind people she'd done back in the second grade. And there was one other haiku that Oggie felt certain he knew who had written:

Ghorks and Shadow Zwills
How you fill my heart with joy
My secret Ghoulers

It had to be Dylan's. Who else would have written about Ghoulers and Ghorks? Each time Oggie visited the bulletin board, his eyes would drift up to the upper right-hand corner where he would reread his own haiku, wondering whether people would recognize the essence of him in the words.

Many of the haiku were hard to match up with a particular person. There was one about riding a bicycle and another about playing with a cat. Pretty much anybody with a bicycle or a cat could have written those. At noon, before the class was dismissed to go to the cafeteria, Mr. Snolinovsky made everybody promise not to discuss the haiku game during lunch.

"I want your guesses to be based only on the poems," he told them. "Not on hints your friends drop about which ones they wrote."

As promised, Amy and Oggie did not discuss the haiku. Instead, Amy quizzed Oggie on the B.P.R.'s while they ate their sandwiches.

"*'Our moon is not cheese, so what's that funny smell?'*" said Oggie.

"No," Amy corrected. "It's not, '*so* what's that funny smell,' it's '*but* what's that funny smell?' Remember? The *b* stands for brain cells."

"Oh, right," said Oggie. "Rule Number Thirty-Five: NO TALKING ABOUT THE THINGS THAT YOUR PARENTS TELL YOU WILL KILL YOUR **BRAIN CELLS**."

"I wonder why you always forget that one," said Amy.

"Probably those fifty-three marshmallows I ate."

"Or maybe the cotton ball." Amy giggled.

As they walked back to class together after lunch, Oggie asked Amy, "Do you think I'll know all the rules by heart by tomorrow afternoon?"

"Absolutely," Amy told him.

"Well, in that case, do you think Donnica likes purses?"

"That's a weird question," said Amy.

"Not really. If I go to the party, I have to bring a gift. My mom thinks I should give Donnica a purse, but I don't even know if she likes purses."

Amy's personal feeling was that the only thing Donnica Perfecto deserved from Oggie was a big fat punch in the nose.

"If she doesn't like purses, I was thinking maybe I could crochet her some pink shoelaces," said Oggie.

"What about Rule Number Two?" Amy reminded him.

"Do you think it would still be breaking the rule if the shoelaces were in a box?" asked Oggie.

Their conversation was interrupted by a loud voice behind them. Donnica was yelling at her friends.

"How many times do I have to tell you? It's not my fault. I told Daddy that the only thing I wanted for my birthday was Cheddar Jam!"

Oggie's eyes got very wide.

Prrrrr-ip! Prrrrr-ip!

"Did Donnica just say she wanted *cheddar jam* for her birthday?" whispered Oggie excitedly.

"That's what it sounded like to me," Amy confirmed.

"What's cheddar jam?" Oggie asked.

Amy shrugged. Neither she nor Oggie had attended the Valentine Dance, so they hadn't heard of the band. Living in Wawatosa, Wisconsin, though, they were used to people trying to come up with new and creative ways to use cheese. But jam? Oggie squinched up his face as he tried to imagine eating a peanut butter and cheddar jam sandwich. It didn't sound very appetizing.

I wonder why Donnica wants cheese for her birthday, Oggie thought. But it didn't really matter. What was important was that Oggie finally knew what Donnica wanted for her birthday, and he made a promise to himself then and there that he was going to get it for her.

Cheddar jam.

15

That afternoon during Creative Writing, Oggie and his classmates made their final haiku guesses. When they were done, Mr. Snolinovsky took the poems off the board and began to read them aloud. The first one he read was typed on a piece of green paper.

I do not know yet
Exactly what it will be
But you will need it.

Amy was the only one who guessed correctly that Oggie had written it. She knew all about Oggie's dreams of being an inventor. Oggie had guessed right about Donnica's and David's and

Bethie's haiku, but to his surprise, Dylan turned out to be the person who had written about the bicycle.

So who wrote the haiku about Ghoulers and Ghorks? Oggie wondered. When Mr. Snolinovsky got to that one and asked the author to stand, Oggie couldn't have been more surprised. But he was not as surprised as the person sitting in the first seat in the third row.

"You collect Ghoulers?!" Dylan cried in utter amazement.

Dylan James had seen the poem on the board and had been waiting on the edge of his seat all day to find out who had written it. Imagine how shocked he was to discover that the one person at Truman who liked the same thing he did was...Amy Schneider. *A girl.*

After school that day, Oggie went to three grocery stores and two cheese shops. He saw cheddar balls, cheddar wheels, cheddar straws, cheddar sticks, and cheddar you could squirt right out of a can. But nobody had heard of cheddar jam. Discouraged, he decided to swing by Too Good to Be Threw and ask for his mother's advice.

"Why do you want to give Donnica jelly for her birthday?" asked Mrs. Cooder.

"Jam," Oggie corrected.

"Are you sure she wouldn't rather have a purse?"

But Donnica had said she wanted cheddar jam. There was one more place Oggie hadn't tried. As he headed out the door to continue his search, a flash of yellow and blue caught his eye and he snapped his fingers as he remembered Dylan's brother's request. A few minutes later, Oggie was walking down the street with a pair of blue-and-yellow-checked pants in Justin's size tucked under his arm.

On his way home, Oggie stopped at the mini-mart attached to the Gas and Go filling station. It was his last hope, but it turned out that the only kind of cheese they had was plain old American, and even that looked a little moldy. Oggie kept his eyes peeled for the Georges and the cherry picker as he continued on his way, but again it seemed they were nowhere in sight. Turk was waiting by the door with his leash in his mouth when Oggie got home, so he dropped his backpack on the kitchen table, hooked the leash on Turk's collar, and the two of them started off toward Walnut Acres to deliver the pants to Dylan's brother.

As he walked his dog, Oggie resigned himself to the fact that he wasn't going to be able to give Donnica what she really wanted for her birthday. He was disappointed, but what could he do? He'd looked everywhere he could think of for cheddar jam, but it was nowhere to be found.

Nobody was home at the Jameses' house. Dylan's bike was gone and there was no car in the driveway. The red trunk was still sitting on the lawn, so Oggie sat down on it and waited for a while to see if anybody showed up. After about ten minutes, he gave up. Before he left, he folded the pants and left them sitting on top of the trunk where he hoped Justin would find them.

That night before he went to bed, Oggie crocheted Donnica a pair of pink shoelaces. He used a ruler to make sure they were both exactly the same length. Maybe he hadn't been able to find cheddar jam, but at least Oggie could make sure that Donnica wouldn't be tripping over uneven shoelaces.

The next morning Oggie awoke feeling nervous and excited. In just a few hours he would be swimming in Donnica Perfecto's pool! He got up and tried to make himself a bowl of cereal, but he was so worked up, first he spilled the last of the cornflakes on the floor and then he knocked over the milk carton. Turk was delighted, and more than happy to help with the cleanup. Oggie had really been too excited to eat breakfast anyway. He looked at the clock. It was only eight fifteen. How was he ever going to last until party time?

At nine o'clock, Oggie put Donnica's shoelaces in a box and carefully tied a ribbon around it. At ten o'clock Mrs. Cooder drove Oggie down to Selznick's department store, where they exchanged his red bathing suit for a yellow one. Oggie also talked his mother into buying him a pair of rubber swim fins he discovered in the sale bin. There was no rule against swim fins on Donnica's list, and Oggie could hardly wait to try them out in the Perfectos' pool. At eleven o'clock, Amy called to quiz Oggie one last time on the rules and to wish him good luck.

"Thanks a BAZILLION for all your help," Oggie told her. "And by the way, how come you never told me you collected Ghorks and Windowsills?"

"They're called *Shadow Zwills*," Amy told him. "And I didn't tell you because I didn't think you'd be interested since you can't play Old Maid with them."

She knew Oggie well.

At twelve o'clock, Oggie was too excited to eat lunch, so he went to his room and *prrrrr-ip-ed* non-stop for an hour and a half. When he was finished, his tongue was completely numb. He tested himself by thinking about piggies-in-a-blanket and he was very relieved to find that he had *prrrrr-ip-ed* himself dry.

It felt like two o'clock would never come, but at last it did. Oggie put on his new bathing suit and got Turk settled in the backyard with a bone to chew on to keep him busy while he was gone. Before he left the house, without even thinking about it, Oggie stopped at the fridge, took out a few slices of American cheese, and slipped them into one of the pockets of his swim trunks.

As Oggie was leaving the house in his bathing suit and swim fins, a familiar white truck came cruising up Tullahoma Street. When it stopped in front of the Cooders' house, Oggie was delighted to see who it was.

"Hi, Georges!" Oggie called to his friends from the phone company. "What are you doing here?"

The two Georges were glad to see Oggie. They explained that they were in the neighborhood because there had been some trouble reported with the phone lines. Oggie remembered that his mother had mentioned something about bad reception only the day before.

"Looks like you're on your way to a party," one of the Georges said, noticing the box with the bow on it in Oggie's hand.

"Yeppers!" said Oggie happily. "It's a swim party and there might even be piggies-in-a-blanket."

"Have fun," they told Oggie. Then Short George climbed into the bucket and Tall George began to raise him up to the phone lines.

As Oggie started flip-flopping across the street in his swim fins, a green van with a watering can painted on the side pulled into the Perfectos' driveway. Several women wearing straw hats climbed out. Oggie waved to them, figuring they were probably relatives of Donnica's who had come to help celebrate her birthday. When Oggie reached the front door, he rang the bell. After a minute, Mrs. Perfecto answered the door.

"Hello," said Oggie, holding out the present to her. "Thank you for inviting me. Here's a gift for Donnica. I made them myself."

But instead of inviting him to come inside, Mrs. Perfecto gasped and put her hands on her cheeks.

"Oh no," she whimpered miserably. "Not now. Not today."

For a minute Oggie thought he must have gotten the day of the party mixed up, but then he noticed that Mrs. Perfecto was looking past him at the ladies in the straw hats. Mrs. Perfecto pushed Oggie out of the way and hurried down the walk, leaving Oggie to show himself into the house.

"Hello?" he called. "Anybody here?"

"Everybody's out back by the pool," came a muffled reply.

At first Oggie didn't see him, because the owner of the voice was sitting on the couch, which happened to be the exact same shade of brown as the fur suit he was wearing.

"Bumbles!" cried Oggie.

The giant bear lifted a paw and waved.

"What are you doing in here?" Oggie asked. "Shouldn't you be outside juggling by the pool?"

"The birthday girl told me to stay inside," said Bumbles. "And it's a good thing, too, because the cleaner shrank my suit and now the eyeholes are in the wrong place. I can't see a thing."

They were interrupted by the sound of a gasp coming from the other end of the room. Donnica, in a pink bathing suit with a terry cloth robe on over it, was standing in the doorway, staring at Oggie as if she were seeing a ghost.

"What are you doing here?" she said.

"You invited me to your party," Oggie told her. "Remember?"

"Of course I remember," she said, "but you told me you had a terrible memory so you couldn't possibly come. *Remember?*"

"I *do* have a terrible memory," Oggie said. "But Amy Schneider and Richard of York helped me, and I memorized every single rule. Want to hear? 'Putting salad under the couch is very messy and dangerous.' Which means no *prrrrr-ip-ing*, no crocheted shoelaces, no Uncle Vern stories . . ."

But Donnica wasn't listening. Her mind was racing a million miles an hour. Oggie Cooder and Bumbles the Bear were both at her birthday party. If she didn't want to be the laughingstock of the entire fourth grade, she needed a new plan and she needed it fast.

16

Donnica wasted no time launching Plan B.

"Quick, you two," she told Oggie and Bumbles. "Follow me. Dawn is upstairs stuck in the bathroom, and you have to help rescue her."

"Rescue Dawn?" asked Oggie.

"Yes," said Donnica. "The bathroom door gets stuck sometimes and the only way to get it open is to push it from the outside. You both have to come rescue her."

"You want me to come, too?" asked Bumbles.

"Uh, *duh*, Yogi," said Donnica. "I said I need both of you, didn't I?"

There was a loud crash as Bumbles stood up, accidentally knocking over a lamp.

"Sorry," he said, trying to pick up the lamp and

in the process knocking a stack of magazines off the coffee table and onto the floor. "I really can't see a thing. I'd take my head off, but I think the zipper's jammed."

"Forget about your head. There's no time for that now. We have to get upstairs!" shouted Donnica.

Oggie tossed the birthday present on the table and grabbed Bumbles by the paw. Together, the two of them stumbled up the stairs behind Donnica.

"Okay," Donnica said when they reached the top of the stairs. "Here's what we're going to do. You two lean against this door, and on the count of three push as hard as you can."

Oggie and Bumbles did as they were told and put their shoulders to the door.

"Ready?" said Donnica. "One . . . two . . . three!"

The minute they leaned against the door, it flew open and Bumbles and Oggie tumbled into the bathroom, landing in a tangle together on the floor.

Knowing she didn't have a second to spare, Donnica pulled the door shut, and using the belt from her robe, she quickly tied the outside bathroom doorknob to the knob on the door of the linen closet right next to it in the hall.

Bumbles and Oggie were trapped in the bathroom!

"What's going on?" Oggie asked as he jiggled the knob in vain.

"Oops!" Donnica yelled through the door. "I guess Dawn wasn't locked in there after all. But now you guys are. Don't worry, though — I'll go find someone to help get you out. I'll be right back."

But Donnica had no intention of coming back. Plan B had worked perfectly. She had Oggie Cooder and Bumbles exactly where she wanted them.

Bumbles and Oggie waited for half an hour for Donnica to return. When she didn't come back, they tried pounding on the door, but everybody was outside in the backyard, and Donnica had turned the music up loud so nobody would be able to hear them.

"I had a bad feeling about this gig from the beginning," groaned Bumbles. "But I need the money. Now I probably won't even get paid."

Oggie climbed up on the edge of the bathtub so he could look out of the window. The green van was still parked in the driveway, but there was no sign of Mrs. Perfecto or the ladies in the straw hats. Across the street, the two Georges were working on the phone wires. Oggie cranked open the window as far as it would go and called out to them, but they couldn't hear him over the loud music that was playing out by the pool, where the party was now in full swing. Oggie sniffed the air and was certain he smelled piggies-in-a-blanket.

"What are we going to do?" Oggie asked.

"I don't know," said Bumbles, "but I'll tell you one thing — if I don't get out of this suit soon, I'm going to burn up. You wouldn't believe how hot it is in here."

Oggie went around behind Bumbles and tried to get the zipper on the bear suit unstuck, but it was no use. It was completely jammed.

"Maybe we should cut the legs off so you can take the suit off from the bottom instead," Oggie suggested.

"Go for it," came Bumbles's muffled reply.

So Oggie found a pair of toenail clippers in the medicine cabinet and began to cut the suit apart. As he clipped away at the brown fur, a familiar flash of yellow and blue caught his eye.

"Hey!" said Oggie. "Where'd you get those pants?"

A few minutes later when Bumbles finally managed to wriggle out of his bear suit, Oggie had his answer: Bumbles the Juggling Bear was none other than Dylan's brother, Justin James.

"Hey, Oggie," said Justin, brushing his long hair out of his eyes and tucking it behind his ears. "I didn't realize it was you out here."

"I didn't realize it was you in there either," said Oggie. "Are you really Bumbles the Bear?"

"The one and only," said Justin. "And it looks like now I owe you two favors. One for the pants and one for getting me out of my costume. Thanks, man. I was really roasting in there. I wish someone would come up with a way to air-condition a bear suit."

Justin reached over and picked up four seashell-shaped soaps that were sitting in a dish next to the sink. At first Oggie thought he was planning to wash his hands, but instead Justin tossed the soaps up in the air and began to juggle them.

"Neat-o!" said Oggie. "I wish I could do that."

"It's easy once you get the hang of it," Justin told him. "I could teach you."

"*Prrrrr-ip! Prrrrr-ip!*" went Oggie.

"Are you okay?" asked Justin, who had never heard anybody make that sound before. "Do you need a drink of water or something?"

"I'm fine," said Oggie. "I just *prrrrr-ip* sometimes when I'm excited. Yellow-bellied sapsuckers

do the same thing — only they say *k-waan k-waan*."

Justin laughed and handed Oggie one of the soaps.

"Okay. Start by tossing this back and forth, from your right hand to your left, until you get the feel of it," he said.

At first Oggie threw the soap too high and too fast, but then Justin explained that it should travel in a slow arc through the air from one hand to the other. Once Oggie could do that, Justin handed him another soap.

"Start with both of them in the same hand," he instructed. "Then throw one and hang on to the other."

This proved to be more difficult to do than it sounded. Oggie tried to throw only one soap at a time, but no matter how hard he tried, he couldn't seem to keep the second soap from slipping out along with the first. Both soaps would fly out in different directions, making it impossible to catch either one. Finally, when one of the runaway soaps went flying at the mirror hard enough to break it, Justin reached out and grabbed it just in the nick of time. The juggling lesson was over.

"Maybe I can teach you later, after we get out of here," Justin said. "Speaking of getting out of here, what do you think is taking so long?"

"I don't know," Oggie said. "Donnica said she'd be right back. You don't think she forgot about us, do you?"

"She better not have," Justin said. "'Cause if I'm not ready to go when the guys get here to pick me up I'm going to be in big trouble. We've got a practice this afternoon."

"We may have to get out of here on our own," said Oggie.

"Got any ideas?" Justin asked him.

Oggie thought for a minute and then he snapped his fingers. Actually, he did have an idea!

17

"How about we cut the elastic out of our underwear and use it to shoot the soaps out the window like my uncle Vern did with his mini-pumpkins?" Oggie suggested. "Somebody will find soap out on the front lawn and figure out we're trapped up here."

"Uh, that sounds kind of weird," said Justin. "Let's see if we can think of a plan that doesn't involve cutting up our underwear, okay?"

Oggie looked around and spotted a basket of wire hair curlers sitting on the counter. He snapped his fingers again.

"These are kind of like the wagon springs Elisha Otis used for his elevator brakes. We could tie them to our feet and jump out the window."

"Uh, that sounds kind of dangerous," Justin pointed out. "And besides, I don't think we can fit through that window. It doesn't open wide enough."

Oggie looked around again. This time his gaze settled on the head of Justin's bear costume.

"*Prrrrr-ip Prrrrr-ip!*" went Oggie.

"Got something good?" asked Justin hopefully.

"Do I ever!" said Oggie. "I just thought of a great invention."

"Will it get us out of this bathroom?" asked Justin.

"Nope, but it will keep you cool inside your bear head." Oggie explained to Justin how his invention would work.

"See, there will be a little fan — the kind that runs on batteries — and an ice bag to lower the temperature of the air. Then you'll have this big rubber band to attach it to your head and, presto, instant air-conditioning!"

Justin grinned.

"That's brilliant, little dude. You should call it

the Cooder Fan. How did you come up with that idea anyway?"

"Necessity is the mother of invention," said Oggie happily.

Justin looked nervously at his watch. "The guys are going to be here any minute. Anybody who could come up with something as great as the Cooder Fan ought to be able to think of a way to get us out of here. Come on, Oggie, *concentrate*."

The last time Oggie had needed to concentrate on something was when he'd been trying to come up with an idea for his haiku. He knew what he had to do.

"Hey, this is no time to be taking a nap," Justin said as Oggie got down on the floor and started folding up the bath mat to make a pillow.

"I'm not taking a nap," said Oggie. He placed the top of his head on the bath mat and pushed himself up into a headstand.

"Trust me," said Oggie. "This is going to work."

And sure enough, it did. Because no sooner

had Oggie turned upside down than a solution to the problem came flying out — of his pocket.

Oggie had forgotten all about the cheese he had slipped into the pocket of his swimsuit.

"Mmmm," said Justin, picking up a slice of cheese and beginning to pull the wrapper off. "I could really use a snack."

"Wait!" cried Oggie as Justin lifted the cheese to his mouth. "Don't bite that!"

"Why not?" asked Justin.

"That cheese is our ticket out of here!" Oggie proclaimed.

As Justin watched in amazement, Oggie began to charve, tilting his head as he went around the curves and picking up speed until he was nibbling so fast his teeth were a blur.

When he had finished, there were three perfectly charved orange letters in Oggie's lap. Two curvy *S*'s and a big round *O*.

"What are we going to do with those?" asked Justin.

"We're going to send out an S.O.S.," Oggie explained. Then he carried the letters over to the window and carefully stuck them backward onto the glass so the message would read correctly from the outside.

Justin was very impressed.

"Like I said, you are one clever little dude, Oggie Cooder. If this works, I'm going to owe you big-time."

Those words were barely out of Justin's mouth when there was a tap on the window.

"You boys need a lift?"

It was one of the Georges. He'd looked across the street and seen Oggie's cheesy S.O.S. stuck to the window and had immediately told the other George to use the controls to send the bucket of the cherry picker over to investigate. Using a screwdriver, he managed to remove the window from the outside, and in no time at all the two boys were clambering into the bucket.

"Oops. Almost forgot something," said Justin,

and he quickly slipped back inside to retrieve his bear suit.

"*Prrrrr-ip! Prrrrr-ip!*" went Oggie as the bucket began to go down.

"You can say that again," Justin said, laughing.

"Okay," said Oggie, and he *prrrrr-ip-ed* again.

The commotion out in the front yard attracted the attention of Donnica's party guests. Pretty soon they were all gathered around the truck watching the rescue.

"Okay, everybody," said Short George as he pulled open the door on the side of the bucket. "Show's over. You boys hop out, and the rest of you move back so we can get this truck out of here."

Donnica, who had just sat down to open her birthday gifts when the excitement began, was furious.

"I will never forgive you for this, Oggie Cooder!" she screamed. "How dare you ruin my birthday party!"

But Donnica's hissy fit was interrupted when Hannah Hummerman suddenly put her hand up to her forehead and began to sway back and forth.

"L-l-l-look!" she said, pointing at Justin with a trembling finger. "It's J.J.!!!"

18

It takes a long time and a lot of hard work to save up enough money to buy yourself a car. But that's exactly what Justin James was trying to do, which is why he bussed tables at the Clam Digger and juggled bowling pins at birthday parties in an overheated bear suit and every now and then showed up at a bar mitzvah or a store promotion or a school dance to play in a rock band called Cheddar Jam.

Hannah Hummerman had been the first to recognize J.J. as he climbed out of the cherry picker in his blue-and-yellow-checked pants, brushing his long blond hair out of his eyes. Soon, all the other girls (and even some of the boys) were going crazy, too. Things got wilder when a beat-up van plastered with bumper stickers pulled up to the curb, carry-ing the rest of the guys in the band.

"Come on, J.J.," one of them called. "Time to rock and roll."

"Cheddar Jam! Cheddar Jam! Cheddar Jam!" the kids started chanting.

Donnica just stood there in her bathing suit with her mouth hanging open.

The boys in the band, enjoying the attention, got out of the van and began to sign autographs on the birthday napkins and scraps of paper thrust into their hands by their starstruck fans.

"I can't believe I didn't faint when I realized that was J.J.," Hannah said to Dawn. "I one-hun-dred-percent guarantee I almost fainted."

Of course, Oggie was surprised to learn that Cheddar Jam wasn't something you spread on bread. No wonder he hadn't been able to find it at the Gas and Go! But even in all the excitement of being locked in the bathroom and rescued by the cherry picker, Oggie hadn't forgotten the promise he'd made to himself.

"Thanks a million, Mr. P," Justin said to Donnica's father as he tossed his tattered bear suit into the red trunk he used to transport his costume and juggling equipment. "This extra cash is really going to come in handy."

Mr. Perfecto felt so bad about what had happened, he'd paid Justin double for the party, even though the only thing he'd juggled that afternoon was the soap in the upstairs bathroom.

"See you later, Oggie!" Justin called as he closed the lid of the trunk and began to lug it over to the van. "Stop by the house any time and I'll give you another juggling lesson, okay?"

Justin slid open the door, and as he and the rest of the guys started to pile in, Oggie knew it was now or never.

"Wait!" he cried.

"What's the matter?" asked Justin.

"I need to cash in those favors," Oggie told him.

Then he took a deep breath and dove in. "See, I never got invited to one of Donnica's parties before, so I wanted to give her something she really, really, really wanted, and when I found out what she really, really, really wanted was cheese jelly, I looked for it everywhere, but I couldn't find it 'cause cheese jelly doesn't even exist, but now that I know that it wasn't really cheese jelly she wanted —"

"Oggie?" Justin interrupted. "I kind of have to get going. Do you think we could talk about this favor you need a little later?"

"Not really," said Oggie. "See, I was wondering if maybe you and your band could play at Donnica's party."

Donnica, Dawn, and Hannah had been listening to this conversation, and when Oggie got to his point, they gasped in perfect unison. Hannah put her hand up to her forehead as if she were going to faint.

"You mean right now?" asked Justin.

Oggie nodded.

Justin had a short powwow with his bandmates in the van and managed to convince them that they could just as easily practice next to the Perfectos' pool as they could in the garage where they usually rehearsed.

When the guys started unpacking the drums and guitars and amplifiers from the back of the van, the crowd of party guests realized what was happening and took up a new chant.

"Og-gie! Og-gie! Og-gie!"

Cheddar Jam set up and plugged in. When they were ready to play, Justin grabbed the microphone and announced —

"This first song goes out to a cool little dude named — Oggie Cooder."

Everybody clapped and whooped. Oggie would have *prrrrr-ip-ed*, but his mouth was too full of piggies-in-a-blanket.

That afternoon Cheddar Jam played every song they knew (some of them more than once), while Donnica's party guests danced and clapped. All Oggie wanted to do was paddle around in the pool, but girls kept asking him to dance, so he'd hop out of the water, dance around in his swim fins for a few minutes, and then dive back in. Oggie was having fun, but he kept wishing that Amy was there, too. Without her help, he would never have gotten to go to the party.

"More piggies-in-a-blanket on the way, you little party animal you!" Mrs. Perfecto called out to Oggie. Her tone of voice was genuinely friendly now. She was in a terrific mood. Not only was her daughter having the best birthday of her life, but Mrs. Perfecto had been invited to join the garden club. In truth, the ladies in the straw hats had been much more impressed with the landscaping across the street at the Cooders' house, but Isabel Cooder had told them that Miriam Perfecto had taught her everything she knew about gardening and that they would be foolish not to snap her up for their club.

"Pssst! Oggie! Over here."

Oggie looked around, finally catching sight of Amy's head poking over the top of the fence. He was so happy to see her, he jumped out of the pool and ran right over.

"I was just thinking about you," he said.

"We came to see how the party was going," said Amy.

"*We?*" Oggie asked.

Suddenly Amy's head started to wobble. Then she started to giggle.

"Dylan's holding me up," she said. "At least he's trying to."

"Hi, Oggie," called Dylan. "How's it going?"

"Good," Oggie called back. "Hey, did you know your brother is Bumbles the Bear and that he's in a band called Cheddar Jam?"

"Of course I knew." Dylan laughed. "He's my brother, isn't he?"

"So what are you guys up to?" Oggie asked. As fun as it was to be swimming in the pool, he realized he kind of wished he could be hanging out with Amy and Dylan instead.

"We're not doing much. Just talking about Ghorks and junk," said Amy. Her head started to wobble again and this time Dylan must have lost his grip because suddenly Amy disappeared completely. Oggie heard the two of them laughing.

"Um, Oggie?"

Oggie turned around and there was Donnica, holding the pink shoelaces in her hand.

"I just wanted to thank you," she said. "For the present."

"You're welcome. I hope you like them," said Oggie. "I was going to give you an old purse, but I decided you might like some pink shoelaces better and I promised myself that no matter what, I was going to give you something that you really, really *really* —"

"The shoelaces are great," Donnica interrupted. "Really. In fact, they're the *nicest* shoelaces I've ever seen. Which is why you'll probably never see me wear them. I wouldn't want to risk ruining something so, um, *unique*."

Oggie smiled.

"Don't worry, Donnica. If you wreck 'em, I can always make you another pair," he said.

"No, no. That's okay," Donnica said quickly.

"One pair is plenty. But really, I just wanted to say thanks, you know, not just for the shoelaces, but also for getting the band to play at my party. That was really nice of you."

Donnica turned to leave, but suddenly Amy piped up from behind the fence.

"Not so fast, Perfecto. Don't you have something else you want to tell Oggie?"

Donnica blushed her favorite shade of pink — bubblegum.

"I'm sorry I locked you in the bathroom, Oggie," she said, hanging her head.

"And?" Amy prompted.

"I'm sorry I made up all those silly rules," Donnica told Oggie.

"And?" said Amy.

Donnica paused for a minute, puzzled.

"What else did I do?" she asked.

"I don't know," said Amy. "But knowing you, I'm sure there's more."

Oggie stayed at the party long enough to sing "Happy Birthday" to Donnica and to eat a piece of cake. He asked Mrs. Perfecto to wrap up two slices to bring to the Georges to thank them for coming to the rescue with their cherry picker. When he got home he was delighted to find Amy and Dylan waiting for him on the porch steps.

"Guess what we figured out?" said Dylan. "You can play Old Maid with Ghouler cards!"

"Yeah," said Amy. "You just have to use a Shadow Zwill for the Old Maid."

"Neat-o!" said Oggie.

They were interrupted by a strange sound coming from the Cooders' backyard.

"*KWEE-URK! Kwee-urk! Week-week wurp-wurp!*"

"What's that?" asked Dylan, alarmed.

Oggie grinned.

"It's a yellow-bellied sapsucker," he told Dylan.

"Yeah." Amy giggled. "A big fat furry one with bad breath."

(Five days later, Turk would surprise everyone by winning first place in the Wawatosa birdcalling contest. It would be the last time he would

compete, however, because when Oggie gave him a big hug to congratulate him, the Swiss Warbler came flying out of Turk's mouth like a rocket.)

That afternoon, after Oggie and his friends had finished playing a few rounds of Ghouler Old Maid out on the porch, Amy suggested that they turn the sprinkler on and run through it to cool off. Even Turk joined in. Next door, Donnica's party was still in full swing. Oggie was glad that she had liked her shoelaces, and that he'd managed to get her Cheddar Jam, even if it was by accident. He had enjoyed finally getting to swim in the Perfectos' beautiful kidney-shaped pool (not to mention all those piggies-in-a-blanket he'd gotten to eat). But that wasn't the reason he threw back his head and let out a loud *prrrrr-ip prrrrr-ip!*

Oggie Cooder was glad to be back on his side of the fence with his friends and his dog and the bazillion other things that made him feel really, really, *really* happy.

Sarah Weeks is the author of over fifty books for young readers. Her titles include *Glamourpuss*, a picture book illustrated by David Small, and the novels *Pie* and *Honey*. Her award-winning novel *So B. It* was adapted as a motion picture, directed by Stephen Gyllenhaal and starring Alfre Woodard and Talitha Bateman. Sarah, a graduate of Hampshire College and NYU, is an adjunct professor in the prestigious MFA writing program at The New School University in New York City. She has two grown sons and lives with her husband, Jim Fyfe, and their dog Mia in a little green-and-yellow house overlooking the Hudson River in Nyack, New York.

Sweet Reads from Sarah Weeks

If Alice didn't inherit her aunt's famous pie recipes, who did? Find out in this delicious story about family and friendship.

★ "An irresistible concoction ...Warm, delicious and filling."
—*Kirkus Reviews*, starred review

Life gets a little sticky when Melody begins to uncover secrets about the mom she never knew, and it suddenly feels like everyone in Royal, Indiana, has something to hide.

■SCHOLASTIC
scholastic.com

WEEKSe